BORN TO
BE WILD

Kris Cassidy

A KISMET ™ Romance

METEOR PUBLISHING CORPORATION

Bensalem, Pennsylvania

KRIS CASSIDY

Kris Cassidy has had a wide variety of occupations including working for NASA, delivering mail and being a successful real estate agent. Through writing she can live many lives, travel all over the world and fall in love over and over again without leaving her home in Colorado. Besides writing (she has published fifteen books since 1985), Kris has appeared as an extra in several movies and on "Wheel of Fortune."

ONE

"You must be the Wild Woman."

Since it was more of a statement than a question, Jennifer Grant almost didn't bother to respond. She was hot, tired, and very worried about the disabled creature that had been demanding her attention for the last half hour. The fierceness of the sun was refusing to show any mercy on either the weakened animal or Jenny as she continued working to keep the dolphin alive.

Briefly glancing up from the dolphin's back to the tanned muscular legs of the man who had spoken, her first thought was that help had arrived, at last. As the stranger fluidly folded his tall frame into a kneeling position in front of her Jenny cast a distracted look at him, noting not his sun-bleached golden blond hair or his vividly blue eyes, but that he had a strong sturdy body with plenty of muscles, which was what she and the dolphin needed most right now.

"Yes, I suppose I am the Wild Woman. At least, that's what a few of the people around here call me," Jenny replied, a friendly smile briefly wiping the worried frown from her face. "But I've always hoped it was a term of endearment because I take care of wild animals. Goodness knows, I haven't done anything else to earn that reputation."

"I can't tell you how disappointed I am to hear that," the man murmured, his voice low and vibrant. "By the way, my name is Garrett Reid. Should I call you Wild, Ms. Woman, or W.W.?"

She couldn't resist a chuckle as she answered, "My friends call me Jenny . . . that is those friends who don't whinny, moo, bark, meow, or cluck."

"Nice to meet you, Jenny," Garrett responded, one corner of his mouth lifting in a charmingly crooked grin. "I've always admired people who were bilingual. I took a few Spanish courses and a little French in college, but I've never met anyone who could speak *barnyard* fluently."

Jenny continued scooping handfuls of water from a small plastic bucket and letting the tepid, salty liquid trickle along the dolphin's silvery-grey head as she spoke with wry candor. "My place is several miles from town or any other ranch, so there are days that go by when *all* I speak is barnyard. Sometimes I think of English as my second language."

He looked at her with an amused curiosity for a

long moment before turning his attention to the dolphin that was lying beneath a protective armor of soaked towels on an unnatural bed of sand. After positioning his own body as a shield to block off as much direct sunlight as possible, Garrett peeled back the wet towels and began giving the animal a thorough and competent examination.

Jenny leaned back and took a well deserved rest as she watched. The sun sparkled in Garrett's bright golden hair while the wind tousled its thickness, spilling a lock boyishly across his forehead. A gaudily colored Hawaiian print shirt covered his shoulders. But its unbuttoned sides flapped in the breeze, making no effort to hide the sexy expanse of sunbronzed flesh on his broad chest above shorts that hugged slim hips.

A twist in the breeze pushed an avalanche of burnished brown curls across her face and she pushed it out of her eyes. This distraction had served to bring her thoughts abruptly back to the situation at hand. Although the man in front of her was obviously much better looking than the dolphin, Jenny was surprised that her mind had wandered in such a strange and dangerous direction.

"Be careful not to pour water down his blowhole or he'll drown," Garrett patiently cautioned a little boy who was dumping the contents of his pail over the shiny mammal. "Do you think you could get that little girl over there to help you bring us some more water? Our friend here will die if we don't keep his body nice and wet," Garrett added in a firm, but gentle voice that sent the boy scurrying away to enlist more members to his bucket brigade.

"What about you?" Jenny asked Garrett. "Are you alone?" Her eyelids flew open as she lifted her gaze to meet Garrett's. "Uh, I didn't mean that the way it sounded. I have a bad habit of blurting out my thoughts, then wishing I had rephrased them first. What I meant to say was that I was hoping Parks and Wildlife would send out several men to help me with this fella instead of just one. It's going to take more strength than you and I have to get Frankie back in the water."

"Frankie?" Garrett questioned as once again he flashed her that funny little grin.

"That's another of my peculiar habits," she admitted, this time without apology. "I have a tendency to name every living creature, as well as a few unliving ones, that cross my path. It seems to give them more of a personality, don't you think?"

"Yes, but why did you choose the name Frankie for our little friend here?"

Jenny's hazel eyes twinkled as she answered. "After Frankie Avalon, of course. I'm a huge fan of old beach-and-bikini movies, so when I saw this fella lying here in the sand, it seemed appropriate to name him Frankie."

"Of course," Garrett echoed with an appreciative chuckle rumbling deep within his chest as he forced his attention away from Jenny's animated expression to the dolphin. "Actually, I'm not with the Parks and Wildlife Department. I'm a marine biologist and I just docked in Corpus Christi last week. They're planning a Sea World-type exhibit named Sea-Free and hired me to advise them. I guess someone from the P and W called them about this guy . . . er, Frankie, because the Sea-Free people contacted me and I came right over." He spoke in a low, mellow tone, as much to soothe the frightened beast as to carry on a conversation with Jenny.

"Well, however you heard about us, and even though there's only one of you, I'm glad you're here," she said, exhaling a grateful sigh. "At least you know something about dolphins. I'm afraid my expertise is limited to land animals."

The dolphin breathed a soft whistling sound as he made a weak movement of his distinctive-shaped head. Intelligent, round, black eyes watched the activity around him, seeming to instinctively trust these people with the soft voices and gentle hands.

Jenny wet a cloth and bathed the creature's grey face. "Poor Frankie. Don't worry, we're going to get you back out into the bay," she whispered sympathetically, then asked Garrett, "Why do you suppose he beached himself?"

"I'm not sure. Other than a few abrasions from the shells, he seems to be in good condition. He's not very old and even though his breathing is slightly shallow, it's probably from the shock. He doesn't appear to be sick," Garrett answered as he continued his careful search. It was obvious that he was as puzzled and disturbed about the situation as Jenny was. "What's this greasy stuff?" he asked, lifting his hand from the dolphin's back and rubbing his thumb over his fingertips experimentally.

"Vaseline. I keep it in my tack box to use on my animals at the shows or on their cuts to protect them from insects. I remembered hearing somewhere that dolphins don't have sweat glands and can't cool themselves off when they get hot and dry. This guy's skin was beginning to crack by the time I got here, and I didn't know what else to put on him to help him." She shrugged, hoping she had not done the wrong thing.

"You did fine," he reassured her with a warm smile. "Dolphins have a thick layer of blubber, covered by a very thin skin that shrinks badly when exposed to air for any length of time. It was essential that he be kept covered and wet, which is exactly what you did. He's not in immediate danger, but he needs to get back into the water as soon as possible."

Jenny's greenish-gold eyes narrowed as she watched the rhythmic rush and retreat of the foam-flecked waves before her gaze swept the almost deserted beach. "I've never seen so few people here. Even though it's the end of May and school's not out for the summer yet, there's usually a handful of kids out here skipping classes. They must be taking final exams or maybe the surf's up at Padre Island and they've all gone down there. It's too bad, we could certainly use a few more muscles." She looked rather dubiously at the little boy, a skinny old man and the young girl he had drafted to help him haul buckets of water from the surf to the beach. She appreciated their enthusiasm, but she doubted that they would be much help when it came to pure brute strength. "And, unfortunately," she continued, "I don't think there's another high tide until after midnight."

"He won't make it until then," Garrett said matter-of-factly, his large hands gently running over the dolphin's smooth skin that felt very similar to a wet rubber ball. "If the water won't come to him, then we'll have to take him to the water. Not only will he overheat, but his weight now that he is non-buoyant could damage his internal organs and cause him to die."

Garrett began rewetting the towels and spreading them back over Frankie's body, but he allowed his gaze to wander from his patient to Jenny. She obviously hadn't planned on spending the day at the beach. Dressed in jeans so old and faded that they were almost white, he knew she had to be very warm sitting out in the blazing sun. Her cotton blouse looked cool and casual, but he could see the telltale moisture of perspiration trickling down her neck and into the shadowed valley between her breasts. He had the impression she was almost to the point of total exhaustion and he began worrying about her almost as much as he was worrying about the dolphin.

"How long have you been out here in this heat? You really should take a break and find some shade or at least put on a hat," he suggested. "Your nose is turning a very interesting shade of red."

"No, I'll be fine," she answered, lifting her heavy hair off the back of her neck so the breeze could cool her heated skin. "It doesn't take much to make my nose pink. It's the only part of me that ever burns. Actually, I've only been here about an hour or so. It's just that I didn't get much sleep last night because one of my horses was sick. And then this morning I had to drive to Victoria to pick up a stallion I had loaned to some friends of mine. I was almost home when I received a call on my CB that someone had reported a dolphin washed up on the beach. So I drove straight here."

He leveled a questioning look at her, one golden eyebrow lifted skeptically. "My expertise is with sea creatures. If you faint on me, I won't have a clue how to revive you short of throwing a pail of sea water in your face," he said, trying not to come on too bossy, but to get his point across with a gentle tease.

"I've never fainted in my life," she exclaimed defensively, then shrugged. "Okay, so I am a little tired. But I'm not leaving until Frankie is swimming out to sea like a good little boy. And nothing you can say or do is going to make me change my mind."

"Stubborn *and* beautiful . . . a dangerous combination," he muttered under his breath as he turned his attention back to the dolphin's situation.

"If only we could rig up some sort of stretcher so we could carry Frankie across the sand," Garrett thought aloud.

"I've got a small tarpaulin in the back of my pickup truck. Maybe if we used it to make a sling, we could pull him back into the water," she suggested.

"That's a good idea, but I don't know if we can move him. He probably weighs between three to four hundred pounds, and you don't look too . . . uh . . ." He hesitated, his eyes sweeping her slender form.

"I'm stronger than I look," she interrupted, lifting her arm and bending it to show a respectable biceps muscle. "I can carry a fifty pound sack of feed or hoist a bale of hay all by myself."

He still looked doubtful, but after a glance around the almost deserted beach was forced to admit, "I guess we don't have a lot of choices. Sure, it's worth a try. Do you need any help with it?"

"No, I can handle it. You stay with Frankie and I'll be right back," Jenny said with renewed optimism as she rose and dusted the sand off her knees and bottom.

Jenny walked as quickly as she could across the deep powdery sand, trying to ignore the grit that filled her tennis shoes, making each step extremely uncomfortable. When she reached her truck, she took a minute to take them off and toss them into the cab before reaching into the back of the truck and dragging out the folded tarpaulin and some rope. Then as a last minute inspiration, she opened the tailgate of the horse trailer, untied and backed out a tiny snow white horse that stood not much taller than her knees.

"Come on, Sugar. I've got a job for you," she said, giving the little horse an affectionate pat before gathering up the tarp and rope, and leading him toward the beached porpoise.

"What the heck is that?" Garrett asked with an incredulous chuckle as the kids squealed in delight.

"This is my horse, of course, of course," Jenny answered in a singsong voice that roughly followed the tune from "Mr. Ed." "Have you been working with fish so long you've forgotten what a horse looks like?"

"I'm from Kansas and the horses we've got back there don't look anything like . . . well sort of, but much, much taller than this one. I've had dogs that were bigger than this little guy," Garrett muttered dryly.

"Well, don't you worry about him. He's stronger than he looks, too," she retorted.

"I hope so because I'll bet this dolphin has him beat by several pounds."

"Don't count us out too soon," she promised with a smug smile. "We'll surprise you, I guarantee."

He had no doubt about that. She was already surprising him on every turn . . . and intriguing him as well. He offered no more protests as he stood up and moved forward to help her unfold the large piece of treated canvas.

They began the tedious process of inching the stiff material beneath the porpoise's heavy body. By the time they had him lying snugly on his hammock, Garrett and Jenny were drenched in sweat and breathing heavily from the exertion. But the most difficult part was still ahead of them. While the children renewed their bucket brigade, the three adults took a well deserved rest.

"You know," Garrett observed as he studied the small inlet that separated the mainland from the long narrow peninsular beach on which they were standing. "The same curiosity that makes dolphins easy to train and domesticate also gets them into a lot of trouble. I think Frankie must have followed something or someone into that little bay and got confused when the tide went out and the channel got too shallow for him to navigate. He could probably hear the sounds of the open sea on the other side of this sand spit and thought he could take a short cut to it. His head is pointing in that direction," he added, gesturing toward the much larger Aransas Bay.

"Then once we get him back into the inlet, what's going to keep him from beaching himself again?" Jenny questioned, noting that there were still no clouds in the azure colored sky to filter out any of the sun's fury and that the tide didn't appear to be rushing any closer than it had been an hour ago.

"It's too far for us to drag him across to the other side and I don't suppose that under these primitive conditions, the trip would do him any good." Garrett rubbed his jaw thoughtfully, frowning slightly as he tried to come up with a solution. "My friend, Pete, might be back from Corpus and if I could contact him, he could get our dinghy and meet us here. Maybe we could lure Frankie through the shallow water and around this sand bar."

"You can use the CB in my truck," she offered. "I'll stay here with Frankie while you try to reach Pete."

"I hope he's had time to get back to the sailboat by now. He was checking on some engine parts or he would have come with me."

A few minutes later when Garrett returned, Jenny had already gone to work fashioning a makeshift harness out of the rope so Sugar could add his strength to the effort.

"Pete's on his way," Garrett announced cheerfully, raking his long fingers through the unruly thatch of hair that the wind had persistently tumbled across his forehead. "Unfortunately, it's going to take him at least thirty minutes, so we're going to have to try and move Frankie on our own. We need to have him in the water by the time Pete gets here so we'll have a few daylight hours left to guide him into Aransas Bay."

"I think we can do it," Jenny reassured him. "You thread that end of the rope through those metal eyes on the tarp and I'll hitch Sugar to this end. If we use the big piling on the end of that fishing pier at the edge of the water, maybe we can rig up some sort of pulley system so he can help us pull."

Garrett looked skeptical, but if he had any further doubts about their probable success, he didn't voice them. Instead he obligingly strung the rope through the tarp, gathering the edges like the drawstring of a purse while Jenny worked on her horse. But even with Sugar's help and the limited assistance of the old man and the two children, it was a real struggle to pull the dolphin's dead weight across the resistance of the soft sand. Ten minutes later, after moving

Frankie only a couple of feet, Jenny let the old man lead Sugar while she joined Garrett to alternately tug and push the canvas wrapped mammal's heavy form.

Even the ever optimistic Jenny was beginning to believe that they would never reach their liquid goal when she felt the welcome tickle of foam curl around her feet, then retreat, leaving the sand beneath her mushy and unstable. With the added handicap of poor traction, their progress was slowed even more than before, but the nearness of success gave them all added strength. As another wave rushed in, Frankie must have felt the gentle pull of the tide and realized how close he was. Eagerly, he twisted, trying to push himself into the water, but the wave had already reversed and disappeared back into the bay.

"When the next wave comes in," Garrett panted breathlessly, "I'll count to three and we'll all give one big push. Okay?" The others agreed with tired nods and together they waited for the next ankle deep swell to approach. "Ready? One . . . two . . . three . . . *push* . . ." he encouraged, digging his heels into the oozy mire, bending over and using the full strength of his muscular body to shove. His face was already bathed in sweat and the tendons of his fore-arms bulged from his effort as they moved forward one step . . . then two . . . and three.

Jenny, too, was putting her entire weight into the job while the old man urged Sugar forward and the children tried to help, but mostly managed to get in the way. Ultimately, it was Frankie who provided the final thrust, wiggling his way out of the tarpaulin sling as the water rose high enough for him to get some buoyancy. The tarp, suddenly limp, washed back at Jenny and Garrett, tangling its heavy wet mass around their legs and pulling them with it when it followed the receding surf. The children, who had been far enough back not to be caught in the mess, scampered back up to the beach, laughing as the two adults struggled to regain their balance. Jenny and Garrett's feet stuck firmly in the sucking sand while their bodies were pulled forward. Like trees being felled in a forest, they swayed, then toppled forward to land face first into the water.

Garrett and Jenny raised themselves up and looked at each other through the curtain of hair that dripped down in front of their eyes.

"We did it!" he gasped triumphantly.

"Of course we did. I never doubted it for a minute," she answered with a wetly brilliant smile that turned into a chuckle, then into a belly laugh which Garrett immediately joined. They sat there, too exhausted to move, laughing until their stomachs ached and tears joined the salty water already on their cheeks.

"After all that work, I needed a bath, but I wasn't quite prepared for this," he finally managed to choke out. Awkwardly, he separated his legs from the sodden tarp and stood up, holding out his arms to help her. She accepted his help, letting her hands be enveloped by his much larger ones.

"Actually things like this seem to happen to me much more often than I'd like to admit."

"Why do I not find that hard to believe?" he teased, his voice suspiciously husky as his gaze strayed to the exciting sight of her thin blouse molding itself wetly to her slender curves. He struggled against his own rising emotions as well as the constant ebb and flow of the tide as he tried to pull her up.

Jenny grasped his forearms to brace herself so she could stand up, but, instead, succeeded in pulling him back down into the surf with her which sent them both back into a fit of laughter.

Again, Garrett staggered to his feet and reached down to help her. As she stood unsteadily in front of him, looking delightfully appealing with water droplets glistening like crystals from her thick, black eyelashes and the long tendrils of her dark brown hair. He was barely aware of his hands sliding up her forearms, over her dripping sleeves until his fingers wrapped around her small, but unquestionably strong biceps.

Jenny's hands rested easily on his denim-covered hipbones. She felt her body sway and weave in rhythm with the waves, but she was also aware of a magnetic pull toward this man that was stronger than the tide. Slowly, inevitably, she let the gentle pressure of his hands and the entrancing warmth of his Paul Newman eyes shrink the distance between them until a mere breath separated his tempting lips from hers.

"Hey, Garrett. Is that the warm-blooded mammal you're needing help with?" An amused male voice carried to them on the wind, startling them out of their intimate mood. Simultaneously, their heads turned toward the open water where a man that could only be Pete threw out the anchor of the small boat he was in, and cut off the outboard motor.

"Great timing, Pete," Garrett called, not loosening his grip on Jenny.

"Nice day for a swim," Pete stated wryly. "But I think you're both a little overdressed."

"Jenny was just washing her clothes and I thought I would join her." Garrett flashed her his fabulous crooked grin as he countered his friend's teasing.

Frankie surfaced between them and the boat, blowing a spray of water away from his blowhole before taking another breath and disappearing beneath the choppy water in a shining silver arc of sinewy muscle. His triangular dorsal fin sliced through the water as he circled the dinghy, obviously playing with his new friends.

"That's the mammal we're here to help," Garrett shouted to Pete. "I hope you have some good ideas on how we're going to convince him he should follow us across that channel."

"How are you at fish imitations?" Jenny asked, her gold-flecked green eyes twinkling. "Unfortunately, that's not in my repertoire of languages."

"Mine either. Of all the courses I took in college, none of them included the study of fish dialects."

"At least you wouldn't have to worry about him mistaking you for lunch since dolphins prefer speckled trout to sunburned toes."

As they joked, Pete had stripped down to a small swimsuit, dived off the dinghy, and was swimming toward them. When he reached water too shallow for him to swim, he stood up and sloshed closer. "Nice to meet you, Jenny," he said. Gallantly, instead of a mere handshake, he lifted her hand to his lips. "I'm Pete, Garrett's best friend and partner. If I had known you were going to be doing your wash, I would have brought a few of my own dirty things along."

"Hey, Sir Galahad. Watch whose hand you're kissing. I saw her first," Garrett warned lightly, but with an undercurrent of seriousness that Pete acknowledged with a mischievous smile, but pointedly ignored.

"I couldn't help myself." Pete shrugged. "That's how I always greet beautiful women who are standing in the ocean."

"Speaking of which," Jenny withdrew her hand, sensing a sudden hint of tension between the two men, "why don't we continue this conversation on the beach? My feet are beginning to wrinkle."

Together they pulled the tarp up on the sand where they spread it out, then folded it into a soggy square. As Pete glanced curiously at the miniature horse, Jenny untied the harness from Sugar leaving only the lead rope fastened to the horse's halter.

"And what is this supposed to be?" Pete asked as he bent down to pat Sugar's soft neck.

"Don't be ridiculous," Garrett scoffed, passing a conspiratorial wink to Jenny. "Any fool can see that that's a horse."

"I've always heard that everything in Texas is bigger." Pete flashed them a bemused look, then changed the subject back to the problem at hand. "I read an article a couple of months ago about some people who lured a trapped whale back out to sea with music," Pete spoke, shaking the water out of his short brown hair. "I brought your underwater speakers and a tape recorder along, but I was in such a hurry, I forgot the tapes."

"I've got several tapes in Bob," Jenny spoke, idly scratching Sugar's pointed, milky white ears.

"Bob?" Garrett and Pete asked simultaneously.

"My truck," Jenny answered matter-of-factly as if it were common knowledge.

"Of course. I should have known." Garrett nodded while Pete rolled his eyes, eloquently implying that he thought they were both crazy.

Jenny led Sugar and the two men followed with the tarp, tossing ideas back and forth as to how they should proceed. After tying Sugar inside the trailer, Jenny went to the truck and flipped open her glove compartment, stepping aside as at least a half dozen tapes, a couple screwdrivers, a flashlight, some loose batteries, several packets of ketchup and salt, and a badly refolded road map tumbled out on the floor.

"Very eclectic taste," Garrett mentioned, retrieving the tapes and inspecting their labels. "The Beach Boys, John Denver, Vivaldi, Huey Lewis & the News, George Strait . . . which do you suppose Frankie would prefer?"

"Frankie?" inquired Pete.

"The porpoise."

Pete shrugged his broad, bare shoulders and threw

up his hands in dismay. He was convinced that Garrett and Jenny had been sitting in the sun much too long.

"Too bad I don't have one of Annette's albums. I'll bet Frankie would like that," Jenny said, her hazel eyes twinkling merrily, then offered, "Why don't you take a variety and see what he responds to best. I wish I could stay and watch, but I have a herd of hungry mouths at home waiting to be fed and my clothes are beginning to feel crispy." She searched under the truck's seat and found a plastic sandwich bag which she handed to Garrett. "Here's something to carry the tapes in to keep them dry. Good luck."

Garrett and Pete waved goodbye and Jenny watched them walk away. She was about to climb into her truck when Garrett stopped and turned around.

"I'll give you a call," he shouted back to her, his voice carrying on the strong wind, ". . . and let you know about Frankie."

Again she nodded. It wasn't until Garrett had waded into the surf and was swimming toward the dinghy with the plastic bag holding the tapes clenched in his teeth that Jenny realized she hadn't told him her phone number or even her last name. And unfortunately, there was no listing in the phone book under "Wild Woman."

Feeling more disappointed than she had reason to, Jenny slammed Bob's door and started the engine. It must be because she would never learn Frankie's fate and that she had lost some of her favorite tapes, she thought, trying to justify her feelings. It couldn't be that she would like to see Garrett again, maybe under more favorable conditions. Could it?

Jenny deftly steered the battered old truck out of the sandy parking area and onto the highway. It was getting late and she should be thinking about how much work she still had to do at the ranch this evening. She didn't have time to worry about the fate of a dolphin or the friendly stranger she had met on the beach.

TWO

It was almost dark when Jenny finally finished her chores and was able to take the long, hot bath her aching muscles needed so desperately. She stretched out in the deep, antique claw-footed bathtub and rested her head on the curved porcelain rim. As her body disappeared beneath a layer of fluffy, iridescent bubbles, she relaxed and let the day's events flicker like a silent movie across the inside of her closed eyelids.

At the time, she had been too busy to pay much attention to Garrett other than how he could help Frankie get back into the water. But now, a few hours later, her subconscious was reviving images of his tall, tanned body and very attractive face with its twinkling blue eyes and seemingly perpetual lopsided grin.

Lord, he had probably thought she was a real loon. He appeared to take it all matter-of-factly, but Jenny couldn't help but wonder what kind of first impression she must have made, tumbling headlong into the surf, pulling this poor man down with her.

Jenny sat up abruptly and shook her head in an attempt to divert the flow of ideas that were flooding into her thoughts. There were plenty of men in her life right now, but they were all either friends or relatives. The sad truth was that there was no one special and there hadn't been for the last six years since she had moved back to Rockport. It wasn't that Jenny enjoyed living alone or that she was excessively difficult to please. It was simply that there weren't very many men who shared her devotion and dedication to animals. If a man didn't understand how important her animals were to her and how keeping her ranch operating successfully was her career rather than merely a hobby, then that man could never fit comfortably into her heart.

Garrett, however, had seemed to be one of those rare men who truly cared for animals, and he also had the added advantage of a friendly, easy-going personality and ruggedly handsome looks that would make any woman stop for a second look. It had been a long time since Jenny had felt her mind wander in such a dangerous direction, but she knew there was little harm in admitting to herself that she would have liked to get to know Garrett Reid better; because, unfortunately, it was unlikely that their paths would ever cross again.

The bath water had cooled off and her bubbles had dissolved into a sudsy foam. Jenny quickly soaped her body, then washed her hair. Pulling the stopper out of the bottom of the tub, she rinsed herself and her long dark brown hair with the clean water that rushed from the crook-necked brass faucet, then wrapped a large yellow towel around her head. After drying off her body, she slipped on a loose light-weight gown.

It was a warm night, and the air outside her open windows hung still and humid while heat lightning danced silently across the clouds. Only the repetitious chirp of crickets and vibrating hum of cicadas, punctuated by the occasional hoot of an owl broke the silence. In most parts of the United States, May was considered to be a spring month. But in South Texas, May was merely a prelude to summer—a reminder of the long, hot nights that would be here all too soon. Jenny cast a wishful glance at the air conditioning unit that sat uselessly in one of the bedroom windows. If only she could spare a few extra dollars this summer, she could get it fixed. She could barely remember the luxury of sleeping in a climate-controlled room. Her house was so small that the air conditioner would effectively cool off the entire building, but it would be specially appreciated at night so she could shut out the ever present humidity.

After drying her hair, she clipped it up on top of her head to keep the heavy silken mass off her neck until she was ready for bed. A glance at the clock told her that it was after ten o'clock, but in spite of her busy day, Jenny was still too keyed up for sleep. She picked up a book she had started reading the night before, but after a few minutes, tossed it aside. It was simply too hot to concentrate. Even the large box fan sitting on a chair in the corner of her bedroom was doing little more than stirring the muggy air which offered minimum relief. Feeling restless and still sort of unsettled after the day's activities, Jenny decided that maybe a cold glass of milk would help her cool off and relax.

Her bare feet padded quietly on the polished oak floors as she walked down the hall and across the living room on her way to the kitchen. Cautiously, she opened the kitchen door, knowing that as soon as she stepped into the room, she would be attacked. As expected, she had barely flipped on the light when twelve tiny, furry feet were scrambling across the tiles toward her. It was a matter of seconds before three fat, fuzzy bodies were rolling and rubbing against her feet and ankles.

Jenny grimaced and bent down to detach one of the kittens' sharp teeth from her big toe. Lifting the tiny animal up, she looked into the kitten's round blue eyes as she scolded, "Shame on you, Tommy. If you don't stop chewing on my toes, I'm going to have to wear boots every time I get around you." The kitten growled affectionately as he stared back at her.

At first glance he might have been mistaken for an

average domestic cat, but the black spots on his back and the abbreviated length of his stubby tail betrayed his true heritage. Jenny tucked the baby bobcat into the crook of her arm as she carefully maneuvered around his two brothers on her way to the refrigerator. These kittens were three of the two dozen or so wild animals Jenny was sheltering on her ranch at the time. Some of the creatures, like these bobcat kittens, were orphaned and needed care and protection until they were old enough to fend for themselves. But most of her wild tenants had been injured and Jenny was doctoring them back to good health so they could be returned to the wild.

Only her miniature horses and a flock of bantam chickens were permanent residents of her Mucho Amistoso ranch. All of the other animals that were now confined in cages, pens, or corrals were merely welcome visitors. As soon as they were healthy and able to take care of their own needs, the wild animals would be set free and the domesticated animals would be put up for adoption. Jenny had long ago learned not to let herself get too attached to any of them because she knew their places in her life were temporary, as was her place in theirs, which was as it should be. It was something she understood as the correct way of nature and had accepted it.

Jenny poured herself a glass of milk and leaned against the edge of the countertop as she drank it. She had taken only a few swallows when from somewhere outside came the sudden noise of her dog's deep, excited barks. At first, Jenny wasn't alarmed because it was not uncommon for possums, armadillos, and even a skunk or two to wander into her yard in search of food, and her dog, Rags, enjoyed chasing them away. Usually, the dog could convince the roaming animal that it would be wiser to keep moving than to stick around. Jenny could tell by the tone of his barks when Rags was playing or when he was seriously attending to his guard duties, and as she continued to listen to him, she began to become a teensy bit apprehensive. When the raucous squawk of a goose who had been disturbed from her rest joined Rags' increasingly frenzied voice, Jenny knew that the intruder must be human.

For a few seconds, she hesitated, trying to decide what action, if any, she should take. Even though her ranch was isolated, several miles from the town of Rockport and over a mile from the nearest neighbor, Jenny didn't usually worry about her personal safety. She knew each rancher and his family in a wide radius in every direction from her house and all of them had more important things on their minds than harming her. This was a small, friendly community whose population generally minded their own business, but who could always be counted on in an emergency.

Jenny was aware that all she had to do was to pick up the telephone and place a call to any one of these neighbors and someone would be there to help her as soon as they could get their pickup truck from their driveway to hers. But even now, with Rags still creating quite a racket, telling her that whoever had dared trespass was still there, Jenny wasn't overly afraid. She had every confidence that she could handle the situation and take care of herself.

Gently setting the feisty kitten back into his wooden box, Jenny tried to remain calm as she outlined her plan of action. First of all, she decided, she would see what all the fuss was about. Flipping a switch, she flooded the yard with light, then pushed aside the curtain on the back window, and peered out. But there was nothing out of the ordinary within her line of vision. Not even Rags was visible. However, from the sounds that echoed hollowly inside the barn, it seemed he had cornered his prey and was holding it in its place . . . which meant that to find out who or what was causing the problem, Jenny would have to leave the relative safety of her house and go outside.

From the row of hooks near the back door, she took a windbreaker and slipped it on over her opaque, but thin nightgown, zipping the light nylon jacket up to her neck. Without socks it was difficult, but she finally tugged on the pair of high-topped black rubber boots she always wore when she was doing chores in the barn. As ready as she would ever be, she stepped to the door. But as her hand curled around the doorknob, she paused again, her gaze lifting to rest on the 20 gauge shotgun that hung on a rack over the coat hooks.

Jenny clearly remembered the day her brother had given her the gun, insisting that she keep it for protection "just in case." She wasn't afraid of guns as long as they were handled properly, and she had practiced with it until she was a crack shot. In this part of the country where the rattlesnakes grew to lengths that were longer than most men were tall, knowing how to use a gun could save her own or one of her animals' lives. But when Jeff had brought her the shotgun, she had laughed, assuring him that she lived so far off the beaten path and had so little of value that she would never have an occasion to use it. Unfortunately, it appeared that now was that occasion.

Carefully, she lifted it off the rack and checked to see that it was ready. Hearing the metallic rasp of the pump as she pushed a shell into the chamber gave her added confidence and she boldly stepped outside, not knowing what to expect. But in the middle of the night on an isolated ranch, a loaded shotgun was an excellent equalizer. She stayed in the shadows as she crept from the house to the barn, her finger hovering near the trigger as she held the gun in front of her.

Trying to be as quiet as possible, she opened the door on the side of the barn and slipped inside. Even though the horses and other animals probably couldn't have cared less, Jenny always left a low-wattage light burning near the stalls. It wasn't very bright, but it illuminated the area enough so that she could see Rags standing in the open doorway of the tack room, his legs spread wide apart as if he were planted to the spot, and the thick, bristly hair on his back standing almost straight up.

Since it was obvious that the intruder was trapped inside the tiny room, Jenny relaxed somewhat. Walking over to the switchbox, she turned on all of the overhead lights and called out. "I know you're in there. If you promise to come out and not try anything foolish, I'll call off my dog."

She waited for several seconds, but there was no answer. "There's no other way out of that room, so you might as well come out now before the sheriff gets here," she continued firmly, hoping her voice didn't betray her little white lie about help being on its way. She was beginning to think she was the one who had acted foolishly by not calling for help before making this attempt to flush out the prowler on her own.

Still there was no reaction from inside the room. Rags tossed Jenny a grateful look over his shoulder, but quickly returned his attention back to whoever or whatever it was that remained out of her sight. Now that she had answered Rags' "alarm," he had stopped barking, but still was uttering an angry growl to remind the intruder whose property this was. But the paradox of the dog's fierce attitude and the lack of response from the prowler was beginning to puzzle Jenny. Perhaps she had jumped to the wrong conclusion and there wasn't a person in there after all. Maybe Rags had been bored tonight and decided to play games with a rat.

She took another step into the room and pulled the chain hanging from the bare overhead light bulb. Automatically, she gasped and retreated as she saw a man pressed into the corner behind a saddle.

"Who are you and what are you doing here?" Jenny demanded unsteadily.

"Please don't shoot," the man answered quickly, extending his hands out in front of him, palms up to show that he wasn't armed.

As he spoke, Jenny noticed that the expression in his eyes was not hostile, but frightened and his tone was not threatening, but almost apologetic. Now that she had taken the time to notice, she realized that "man" wasn't exactly the correct term for the person in front of her. "Boy" would be more like it. Although he was several inches taller than she was, she guessed that he couldn't be much older than seventeen or eighteen. And it was obvious that he was more afraid of her than she was of him.

The boy's gaze travelled from her face to the gun, on to Rags' still aggressive stance, then back to Jenny. Swallowing visibly, he continued, "I didn't steal anything. I promise. I haven't touched a thing."

"Then what are you doing in my barn at this time of night?"

The boy ducked his head as if he were reluctant to answer her question. When he spoke again, he couldn't quite meet her eyes. "I was on my way to Houston when my car broke down. I've been walking for miles, but when I couldn't find a service station and I saw that big storm brewing, I figured I'd better find some shelter for the night. I wasn't going to take anything," he repeated.

Jenny's gaze swept around the small room, noting the makeshift bed that had been neatly laid out with thick, padded saddle blankets for a mattress, lighter weight horse blankets for covers, and a stuffed backpack for a pillow.

"But, hey, I didn't mean to cause any trouble." The boy picked up the blankets, shook the hay off them and hung them back on their racks, then swung the backpack over his shoulder. "I'll hit the road and make a few more miles before the rain starts."

Jenny's heart went out to this prickly, yet somehow pathetic kid. Her instincts about human and animal nature were generally pretty good, and in this instance, although she didn't believe his story about the car, she believed he had meant no harm and was simply trying to stay dry and be as comfortable as possible under the circumstances. She suspected he was a runaway, escaping from some real or imagined teenage crisis, taking temporary refuge in her barn. There were many times that she had spent the night out here herself, waiting for the imminent arrival of a newborn animal or watching over one who was critically ill. However, her discomfort on those occasions had been her own choice and not because she thought she had no better place to sleep.

"I didn't say you had to leave," Jenny said gently. "It's too late for you to get your car fixed. There aren't going to be any service stations open around here at this time of night and that storm is going to hit soon." As if on cue, a flash of lightning illuminated the barnyard, quickly followed by a rumble of thunder that shook the old building's wooden rafters. "You're welcome to spend the night here as long as you don't leave any of the gates open or smoke in here.''

A little of the defensiveness faded from the boy's dark brown eyes. ''I don't smoke and I wouldn't do anything to harm your animals. I've never seen such neat little horses.''

''Good, then it's settled,'' Jenny replied positively. ''And I'll bet you're hungry. Why don't you remake your bed and I'll see what I can find in my refrigerator.''

''Nah, I'm not hungry,'' the boy responded, as he let his backpack slip back onto the hay.

''It's no trouble. I hate to throw my leftovers away and I'm sure there's something in the frig that you could clean up for me,'' Jenny persisted, hearing the insincerity in his protests.

''I guess I could eat a little something,'' he agreed almost too eagerly. ''I don't have much money with me, but I'll do some work for you tomorrow to pay for it. I'm good with animals and with all the ones you've got around here, surely there's something I could do to help. In fact, I maybe could stay a couple of days if you needed me.''

Jenny's smile faded slightly. As much as she wanted to help this boy, she didn't know what she could do for him. Containing only three hundred and twenty acres, Mucho Amistoso was a small ranch compared to the multi-thousand acre ranches that surrounded it. In this part of Texas the soil was rich and fertile, but unless it was properly cultivated and irrigated, only mesquite and cactus would grow.

When it came to taking care of herself and her animals, Jenny was very competent, but her talents did not include farming which meant that the land was costing her more than it was earning. Most of the income was brought in by the sale and stud of her miniature horses. But it, as well as the small allowance she was paid by the Texas Department of Parks and Wildlife for her boarding and veterinary expenses of the wild animals, went directly back into the operational costs of the ranch. It barely supported her, so how could she begin to consider adding another mouth to her already stretched-to-the-limit budget?

But as Jenny looked at the hopefulness that had crept into the boy's eyes, she didn't have the heart to turn him away. From his tone of voice, it had been a long time since he had felt anyone needed him for anything. Surely she could find something for him to do to make him feel he was earning his keep while she did a little investigative work about finding out who and what he was running away from.

"I'm sure you could be a lot of help . . . ?" Jenny hesitated when she realized how very little she knew about this boy. She didn't even know his name! Lord, she hoped she wasn't making a rash decision she might later regret, but it simply was not in her nature to turn out any stray . . . whether it was animal or human. As the literal translation of her ranch's name "much friendly" implied, Jenny's open-door policy was the basis on which it had been established.

"My friends call me Rusty."

"Okay, Rusty. Make yourself comfortable and I'll go see what I can put together. It won't be as good as Whataburger, but it will be filling."

"Hey, that's fine. I had a hamburger for lunch." For the first time, a tentative smile lifted the corners of Rusty's lips. "And thanks, Mrs. . . ."

"It's Miss, but my friends call me Jenny," she replied with a wide, friendly smile of her own. Shifting the heavy shotgun from her right hand to her left, she whistled for Rags and left the barn.

Five minutes later, Jenny returned with a plate filled with sandwiches, a canned soft drink, and a bag of potato chips. She had taken time to change into a pair of jeans and a T-shirt before putting together the impromptu meal, and, in a show of trust, she had left the gun behind in the house.

Jenny watched as Rusty devoured the food with typical teenage gusto, proving that he was hungrier than he had wanted her to believe and reassuring her that she was doing the right thing to let him stay for a few days. She had never refused hospitality to anyone or anything who had found its way to her door. Of course, most of her charges were brought to her by people who couldn't, for one reason or another, take care of the animal themselves. But, as if through some sort of mysterious intuition, there was also an amazing number of creatures who were drawn to Jenny's helping hands and generous heart. Rusty fell into this latter category. And, like all the rest of her visitors, he would leave eventually—as soon as someone wanted to adopt him. But, as with any stray, be it animal or human, Jenny felt it was her responsibility to make them as comfortable as possible during their stay with her.

"There's a storage room attached to the back of the garage that should be more comfortable for you than the barn," Jenny announced as Rusty let Rags clean the last crumbs off the plate in a sort of peace offering. "When my grandparents got too old to handle all of the chores alone, they would hire a college student to help them out and they let him live out there. It has a bathroom, a small stove, a compact refrigerator, and a few other pieces of furniture including a bunk bed. I'm sure it will take some cleaning though, because no one has used it for anything but a junk room since my grandfather died several years ago. If you could manage to be comfortable here in the barn tonight, tomorrow we can take a better look at the garage and see what all needs to be done."

This time the grin that stretched across Rusty's face was completely relaxed. "Hey, that'd be terrific. It'd be nice to have someplace to crash for awhile. . . . er, until I get my car fixed, that is."

Jenny returned the smile with a confidence she did not feel. She couldn't help but think that perhaps this time she had taken on more than she could handle. This was one of those moments when all of her responsibilities seemed to press down on her until she felt as if she were suffocating. She enjoyed being independent, living the life she chose to lead, but sometimes she worried that she might not be able to make it on her own. There was the expense, the headaches, and the work, but there was a tremendous sense of self-satisfaction, too.

Bidding Rusty goodnight, Jenny ran across the yard, trying not to get soaking wet from the rain that was now pounding down from the pitch black sky. The storm had finally arrived, fulfilling its earlier promise of nastiness. Even Rags had decided not to brave the elements, but to stay behind in the comfort of the barn with his newfound friend.

Jenny locked the door behind her and switched off the lights as she left the kitchen and headed toward her bedroom. Perhaps things wouldn't seem so overwhelming or so difficult if she had someone willing to share the load with her. None of the men she had dated since college had seemed interested in anything but their own careers and sexual pursuits. None of them found the relatively quiet lifestyle or never ending work on the ranch appealing.

For some inexplicable reason, a vision of Garrett Reid's gentle hands examining the dolphin crossed her mind, followed quickly by a memory of Garrett's charmingly crooked grin and the ridiculous sight of him sitting, fully dressed, in the surf with waves crashing over his head. Now there was a man who wouldn't mind staying up all night bottle feeding an orphaned litter of coyote pups or spending the afternoon shoveling horse manure out of the barn.

With a disgusted snort, Jenny pulled the barrette out of her hair and shook the silky mahogany colored tresses until they fell loosely around her shoulders. As she dried off and got ready for bed, she wondered why she couldn't get that man out of her mind. There were too many other things to worry about and she was wasting her time thinking about someone she barely knew and would never see again. In spite of her weakness for trying to take care of every forlorn creature who landed on her doorstep, Jenny was painfully realistic and always practical.

THREE

Jenny adjusted the crescent wrench until it clamped firmly on the faucet handle. The metal of the pipe was old and corroded by the high mineral content of her well water. She tugged and pulled, trying to get enough leverage to make the most of her limited strength. At last it moved and after a few more turns of the wrench, she broke the weathered seal and finished unscrewing it by hand.

Even if she hadn't had to struggle so much to free the faucet, it was one of the hottest days so far this month, and it didn't take much effort to work up quite a sweat. With the back of her hand, Jenny wiped her forehead, pushing aside her wet, dark brown bangs. The cool water that trickled from the open end of the pipe felt good against her heated skin and she couldn't help but think about how good a swim in the ocean would feel right now. However, she hadn't been able to find time to get away from the ranch long enough for that frivolity since . . .

Jenny's thoughts drifted back to the last time she had felt the refreshing water of the ocean sweep around her body. The memory was both good and bad. It had been more than two weeks since that bizarre day when she had spent the afternoon with a beached porpoise and a charming marine biologist.

Unfortunately, she didn't know the fate of either. Hopefully, Frankie was out in the Gulf of Mexico chasing little fish and flirting with female dolphins. And Garrett was probably doing much the same thing, except that he was studying little fish and flirting with local beauties. Which, after all, wasn't really any of her business, Jenny reminded herself. Garrett was footloose and fancy free, and obviously happy with his lifestyle, just as Jenny was with her own. Perhaps someday a wonderful, eligible man would find his way to her doorstep just as everything and everyone else seemed to do.

Which reminded her about her latest stray, Rusty. As promised, he had spent several days cleaning the storage room until it fairly sparkled. Then he had turned his attention to sorting and rearranging the garage that contained, if possible, even more clutter than the storage room, Instead of piles of tools on the tables and in boxes, each hammer and screwdriver now hung in neat rows from pegboards Jenny hadn't even known were affixed to the walls. Screws and nails had been assorted by size into jars and all the trash had been hauled away.

So far Jenny hadn't regretted her decision to let Rusty stay at the ranch. She had to stretch her grocery dollars a little farther because teenage boys' appetites were legendary, but it was sort of nice to have someone around to talk to and help her with the chores.

Not that he was much help today. Unfortunately, he knew even less about plumbing than she did, which was next to nothing, she thought wryly as she turned her attention back to the task at hand, threading the new faucet onto the old pipe. But with the help of a do-it-yourself plumbing repair manual, she was doing an adequate job and saving the considerable amount of a plumber's bill. She had just picked up the wrench and tightened it to the pipe when the sound of an engine roaring up her driveway was quickly followed by the vociferous chorus of several of her animals. It was always a chain reaction, started by Rags' deep, staccato bark, followed by the screeching honk of her goose, then her chickens, goats, a burro, and eventually, her horses added their own particular harmony. It was as if they all felt obligated to join in the effort to notify her that she had a visitor.

However, many people didn't know quite how to react to such a boisterous welcome. Not knowing that it was more enthusiasm than viciousness, most strangers waited to get out of their cars until Jenny greeted them personally.

She wasn't expecting anyone, but visitors didn't always call before dropping by, especially neighbors. And from the sound of the vehicle, Jenny guessed it was a motorcycle rather than a car which meant it was probably a local and not an out-of-towner or tourist dropping by to view her "zoo."

As Jenny tried to unstick her rubber boots out of the gooey mud puddle that had been made by the leaky faucet, she cast a worried glance toward the garage. She had repeatedly cautioned Rusty about remaining out of sight whenever strangers came to the ranch. It wouldn't be beneficial for him or her if he were discovered staying at Jenny's ranch. She was afraid she would be accused of harboring a runaway before she had had a chance to help the boy.

It unsettled her nerves even more when she heard a man's voice calling, "Is anyone home?"

Her heart leaped into her throat. It was Garrett! She had only heard his voice that one day, but she would have recognized it anywhere. How had he found out where she lived? What was he doing here? And why, for goodness sake, hadn't she taken a little more care with her appearance? She looked down with dismay at the yellow tank top and faded cut-off blue jean shorts that were both dotted with mud and other, more unpleasant stains that one picks up around a barnyard. Even though she knew it was useless, she tried to smooth back strands of hair that had escaped from her ponytail and insisted on curling loosely around her face.

"Oh, there you are," he stated cheerfully as he walked around the side of the barn and found her. "I know I said that you should dress casually for our date, but isn't this a little too casual?" One corner of his mouth tilted up in that teasing, crooked grin that she remembered too well and his twinkling blue eyes surveyed her disheveled appearance from the top of her tousled head to her mud-caked rubber boots.

"Date? What date?" she managed to ask, her confusion at his statement overcoming the surprise of his visit.

"I left a message with your brother that I'd be by this afternoon around six to return your tapes and that I hoped you would take pity on a lonely out-of-towner and let me take you out to dinner tonight." He glanced at his watch, then back at her obviously underdressed figure and his smile faded slightly. "It's almost six. Should I take this as a 'no' to my invitation?"

She made a mental note to have a talk with Rusty about his memory . . . or lack of one. For a second she considered telling Garrett that the person he had spoken to hadn't been her brother, but that would lead to further explanations which she didn't think he would understand or want to hear. After thinking about what she would do differently if she were to see Garrett again, now that he was actually here, wanting to take her out, she didn't want this evening to start off on the wrong foot. Jenny didn't have to think twice before saying, "I'd love to go to dinner with you tonight. It's just that I wasn't expecting to see you again . . . er, today. I've been working out here in the barn all afternoon and haven't gone to the house to check for messages. But I'm not sure if you want to wait for me. I'm afraid it's going to take me quite a while to shower and change, and I've got to finish this first."

"I've got the whole evening free, so I don't mind the wait as long as I get to eat sooner or later. It seems that whenever I'm on a job in a strange city, my schedule gets so tight that I forget about meals until it's too late to go out to eat. And I'm not a terrific cook," he answered with a chuckle.

"Neither am I," Jenny responded matter-of-factly, his honesty drawing out her own admission. "I can whip up an excellent hot mash for the horses or throw together a fine meal for a family of possums, but when it comes to cooking dinner for myself, I've learned how to microwave or open cans."

Garrett took a few cautious steps closer to see what she was doing. "So what if you're not a gourmet cook. It looks like you have more than your share of talents . . . and apparently plumbing repairs is one of them. Do you need any help?" But his question was, for the most part, rhetorical. He didn't know enough about plumbing to fill the pockets of the white slacks he wore, but he certainly could hold a wrench, turn a handle, or, as a last resort, help call a plumber.

"No, thanks. I'm almost through. I just had to replace this faucet. It froze up last winter and must have cracked. It started leaking a few days ago, and, as you can see, has made quite a mess. I wanted to fix it before my whole barnyard became a pig pen.'' She finished tightening the fitting and checked to make sure the handle was turned off. ''Would you mind turning the main valve back on? It's the blue knob on the well over in the front corner of the barn.'' She pointed one mud speckled hand in the general direction of the well to which she was referring.

''Sure, I believe I can manage that,'' he answered and disappeared around the corner heading toward the front of the barn.

A few seconds later, she heard the pump start up and water surge through the empty pipes. Waiting a little longer to see if any leaked out, she turned the handle and watched with satisfaction as the water rushed out, then stopped completely as she turned it back off.

''Well, I'm impressed,'' Garrett chuckled. ''You must be pretty handy with those tools. I admit that I wouldn't have known where to start such a project.''

''Neither would I a few years ago. But I had to learn. If I had to call a repairman out here every time something broke, I wouldn't be able to afford groceries.''

''Speaking of groceries, where would you like to go for dinner? I'm afraid I've been so busy with the project that I haven't had time to find any good places on my own.''

Jenny walked out of the mud, her boots making slurpy sucking noises until she reached the drier, hard-packed dirt. "There's quite a few fast-food places in town and a couple of nice restaurants that serve a variety of dishes. I'll eat almost anything except raw fish . . . oh, but I suppose you wouldn't eat raw fish either, would you?"

"Some of my best friends are raw fish," he joked.

"Come on in the house and I'll get you something cold to drink while you wait for me to clean up."

Garrett held the gate open for her, then followed her up the path to her small frame house. He was more than interested in the pleasant view of the lovely female in front of him. Tall and slender, her body swayed with an unconscious sensuality as she walked. Even though her clothes were dirty and obviously not new, they showed off her figure to its best advantage. He had always been a sucker for tight, short shorts and Jenny's legs were just perfect for them. He felt a wave of heat rush through his body, an automatic response to a desirable woman. And knowing this lady was no weak, helpless female made her no less feminine and attractive to him. In fact, that, more than her appearance, had kept his thoughts returning to her time and again during the last two weeks.

Even though he had been extremely busy pushing Sea-Free from the planning stages into a reality, he would catch himself thinking about Jenny, wondering if she could possibly be as caring, delightful, funny, and attractive as he remembered. Their meeting had been so brief, yet eventful, that it confused his memory of her until he began to believe that he must have exaggerated her good qualities and overlooked her bad. He had met several women who lived or worked much closer to the site of Sea-Free and who had let him know in no uncertain terms that they were interested in getting to know him on a more personal basis. But he met women like those in every port where he had ever docked and they didn't interest him.

However, Jenny did. She wasn't the average, bikinied, beauty queen type who hadn't had an original thought in years that usually hung around these coastal resort areas. So yesterday, Garrett had finally decided that enough was enough and the only way to find out if Jenny was as wonderful as he remembered, would be to see her again. It hadn't been difficult to track down a game warden who knew her address and could give detailed directions to her ranch. During the course of the conversation, Garrett had also discovered the interesting and possibly useful information that she wasn't married and had been living alone in a small, run-down house miles out in the country, for the last five or six years, and that she was well liked and respected by everyone who knew her.

He found it puzzling that someone like Jenny wouldn't have men camping on her porch, begging for her attention. Well, tonight he would find out why. There must be something wrong with her that he hadn't yet discovered. Maybe she ate with her elbows or drank too much, and soon he would see for himself.

"Be careful not to let anything that's in get out, or anything that's out get in," she cautioned as she opened the screen door and stepped into the kitchen.

Garrett cast her a confused look, but quickly understood her meaning as the dog and the goose who had noisily greeted him in the driveway tried to sneak inside before he could close the door and three tiny odd-looking kittens dashed between his legs and began climbing up his pants in an attempt to get outside. Pulling the door shut quickly, he bent down to pick up one of the kittens, carefully disentangling the baby's sharp claws from the material of his slacks as he inquired, "I'm almost afraid to ask, but what are you doing with a litter of bobcats?"

"Their mother was hit by a car, so a friend of mine at Parks and Wildlife brought them to me to raise."

Wiggling his finger in front of the kitten's face, Garrett laughed at the tiny animal's fierce concentration. "I never realized baby bobcats were so cute. They're even playful like regular kittens. What are you going to do with them when they get a little older? I'll bet you wouldn't have any problem selling them."

"Oh no," she stated vehemently, shaking her head and sending her long ponytail whipping around her neck. "When they're old enough to take care of themselves, I'll take them out to a private ranch or an animal preserve here in South Texas and let them loose. Besides, it's illegal to keep a wild animal in this state without a permit. Not that I would ever sell one, even if I could. They don't make good pets because they never truly adjust to domestic life.''

''You mean all those animals out there in your backyard are eventually going to be released back into the wild?''

''All of the wild ones, except that stupid goose who refuses to leave.''

''Yes, I believe I met your goose. She's a better watchdog than your dog.''

''I know. She's very protective. That's one of the reasons I named her Mother.''

''Mother Goose?'' Garrett repeated with a groan.

Jenny chuckled. ''She's not too good with stories, but whenever someone comes into my yard, she squawks loud enough to wake the dead. A careless kid with a .22 rifle shot her in the wing a couple of years ago, and even though it's completely healed, she seems to have forgotten that she's a Canadian goose and is supposed to migrate north in the spring. In fact, I'm afraid she thinks she's a German Shepherd, but it's something we've all learned to live with. I can't afford to get her psychiatric help . . . not that a goose shrink would be easy to find, even if I tried.'' Jenny opened the refrigerator door and took out a container of premixed formula and poured it into three clean bottles. Setting them in a microwave, she turned the timer to twenty seconds and pushed the COOK button. ''What can I get you to drink?'' she asked, turning her attention back to Garrett. ''Iced tea, Coke, or water?''

"Whew!" he breathed an exaggerated sigh of relief. "For a minute there, I was afraid you were going to offer me one of those." He nodded towards the microwave whose timer had just buzzed.

Jenny took the bottles out of the oven, screwed on elongated nipples and tested them for warmth on the inside of her arm. "Don't be silly. The good stuff is for the babies. It contains no sugar, caffeine, artificial color, or any of those other things that are probably bad for you."

"Well, you've talked me out of a soda or tea. Could I have a glass of ice water?"

"Sounds good to me," she answered, putting some ice in two glasses and filling them from a large jug of water in her refrigerator. Handing a glass to Garrett she set a baby bottle on the table next to him and asked, "Here, would you mind feeding Tom while I take my shower and then I can help you with Dick and Harry? Tommy is the most impatient one and if he isn't fed first, he'll chew on your feet, shoes, ankles, or whatever else he can stretch his mouth around."

"Sure, just show me how to do this. I've had no experience with babies, except the underwater-type, none of which have ever required me to bottle-feed them. Now if you had handed me a bucket of chopped squid or mullet, I would have felt right at home."

Jenny smiled as he put down his glass and picked up the bottle. The kitten immediately grabbed the nipple and started sucking, obviously needing no help at all. "See, you're doing fine. Just don't hold them on their backs like human babies or they might choke. Animals usually eat right-side-up. If Tommy finishes before I get back, feel free to start with either of the other two. I'll try to hurry."

While she was gone, Garrett looked around the tiny kitchen. His mother had once told him that a man could learn the most about a woman by looking at her kitchen. He had always thought that was strange, mainly because most of the women he dated had perfect, *Good Housekeeping* type kitchens, complete with a Cuisanart, wok, electric can opener, a vita-master, and all the other latest state-of-the-art appliances lined up along sleek countertops. They all seemed to be cut from the same mold.

But Jenny's kitchen was different. There was no cutesy wallpaper cluttered with flowers or fruit. Instead the walls were painted a cheery yellow. Light, lacy curtains fluttered in the breeze at the open windows and the black and white linoleum floor was scuffed and worn, but sparkling clean. Except for the microwave and what looked like a tiny spaceship, but was probably a compact incubator, there were no other appliances on the tile countertop. A dishdrainer sitting next to the sink held several more baby bottles, two plates, two glasses, and two sets of eating utensils. An old-fashioned almanac calendar hung on one wall and a coat rack with dog leashes, a yellow raincoat, a windbreaker, a bridle, and a battered straw cowboy hat hung beneath a gun rack near the back door. But instead of looking spartan, there was a homeyness, a warmth that made him instantly comfortable there. He could feel Jenny's friendly, casual personality all around him.

Besides the most basic kitchen appliances and cabinets, the room was barely large enough to hold the small square table at which he sat and a wooden apple crate in the corner that was lined with a blanket that had been shredded by three sets of tiny claws. He could almost smell homemade bread, fresh pumpkin pies, and a goose . . . er, turkey roasting on Thanksgiving Day. This room was a place for mothers and grandmothers, chocolate chip cookies, frecklefaced kids, and drippy purple popsicles.

"Ouch!" he exclaimed as the kitten turned his attention from the empty bottle to Garrett's thumb. "I guess that means you're through, eh, Tom?" he chuckled, holding the little bobcat more snugly and lifting it up so he could see the fuzzy, wide-eyed face. "Am I supposed to burp you now? Is that what your real mommy would do, little fella? No, I guess not, but I can at least wipe the milk off your mouth. What a messy guy you are."

"You're a natural foster parent," Jenny laughed from the doorway. "He didn't receive so much attention from his own father."

Garrett looked up at her, the tilt of his golden eyebrows evidenced his surprise. "That was quick. I didn't realize women could get dressed that fast. And . . . what a change . . . you look terrific!"

Jenny pretended to be insulted. "Was that a compliment? Please let me know because I have a tendency to miss those sneaky ones.''

"No, I mean, yes. Wait a minute," he sputtered. "It's just that you were so quick. I don't mean to sound sexist, but most women take forever just to put on their lipstick. And here, you've showered, fixed your hair, and dressed. What sort of magical bathroom do you have, anyway?"

"No magic," she laughed, pirouetting so that the full gathered skirt of her white cotton sundress swirled around her long, bare, golden-tanned legs. Her thick, shining hair fanned out before settling softly around her shoulders and her cheeks were flushed with a healthy glow. "Just a blow dryer, a little natural curl, and a closet with limited selections, so it never takes me long to decide what to wear."

"Well, it's a magical combination," he replied, setting Tommy on the floor and standing up. He had known the room was small, but suddenly he was close . . . much too close to Jenny for his peace of mind. He could smell the clean fragrance of shampoo and a light floral perfume that radiated from her. As if his hand moved of its own accord, it lifted to touch the irresistible silkiness of her dark mahogany colored hair, pushing it back from her face. "You look absolutely beautiful, even when you're standing knee-deep in mud and have smudges on your nose. But this is the first time I've seen you dressed up, and . . ." His voice lowered huskily, "you take my breath away."

As if her body were still being lifted and moved by the waves, Jenny felt herself swaying toward him. She could feel the heat of his breath on her face just seconds before she nervously took a step backward.

He's only teasing you, Jenny told herself as she picked up a baby bottle in one hand, a kitten in the other, and with shaking fingers busied herself feeding Harry. This is probably the line Garrett uses on all his conquests, she thought, but God help her, it was working. This man could be dangerous to her hard-fought independence and self-sufficiency. It would be so easy for her to like him very much . . . too much. But soon, probably only a couple of months or maybe even weeks, he would be sailing away to a new assignment and a new woman. Jenny couldn't let herself care too much or she would be hurt when he was gone.

It was like her wild animals. She had to feed them and doctor their wounds, but no matter how cute they were, or how much she enjoyed having them with her, she knew better than to get too attached to them because when they were ready, she would have to let them go. It was a lesson she had learned the hard way. She must make the most of each moment because as inevitably as the sea pounded against the shore she would be the one who was left behind.

"These three guys are going to go into cages outside next week when they switch to solid food," she said aloud, abruptly changing the subject to a safer one. "They're getting too mischievous to keep in here much longer. I've already had to put my tablecloth away because they kept pulling it off. And even though it cuts off circulation through the house, I have to keep the kitchen door shut so they can't wander into other parts of the place. Not to mention, that cleaning litter boxes is not one of my favorite chores.''

Garrett looked down at his foot where one of the kittens was balanced on his shoe, batting the shoe strings with its paw. Following Jenny's lead, Garrett picked up the remaining bottle and the last kitten. So it hadn't been the sun that had dazzled him on the beach that day two weeks ago. He had sensed it then and the feeling was even stronger now—Jenny was a very special lady, one whom he would definitely like to get to know much better. But she was obviously as skittish as a newborn filly and he knew it would be wise to try to keep things light between them . . . for a while anyway.

''How did it go with Frankie after I left?'' Jenny asked.

''The music worked great. He followed us around the point and out into the Gulf.''

''Which tape did he like best? No wait, let me guess. Was it the Beach Boys?''

Garrett shook his head. ''No, for some reason he seemed to prefer John Denver over all the rest.''

''So do I,'' Jenny agreed. ''I should have guessed he would like 'Calypso.' ''

''Actually, his favorites were 'Thank God I'm A

Country Boy' and 'Rocky Mountain High,' " Garrett informed her with a laugh.

"It sounds like Frankie might have an identity problem," she commented wryly.

"Which could explain his sudden urge to take a walk on the beach."

"Perhaps we can find a psychologist who treats both geese and dolphins," she added.

"But I thought you might like to know that he had someone waiting for him, probably his Annette. They had a very joyful reunion and were last seen splashing into the sunset."

"I love happy endings, don't you?" But she couldn't help thinking that it was too bad they didn't happen more often.

A half hour later, Garrett and Jenny were on their way to the not-so-large town of Rockport. They had mutually agreed that riding in Bob, however ancient and unsightly the truck might be, would be more comfortable than riding double on Garrett's candy apple red Honda Elite motorcycle. "It's the only land transportation I can carry on my sailboat," he had explained. "Besides, it's cheaper than renting a car in every city where we dock. I usually get so involved in my projects that I don't stray far from the site whenever I'm working."

"And, of course, you can always find a willing volunteer to chauffeur you around in her car wherever you are," Jenny said and was immediately sorry that she had spoken the remark out loud. What possible difference could it make to her what his mode of transportation was . . . or with whom?

"Yes, this is just one of the many perks that go with my job," Garrett declared, as he patted Bob's cracked and faded dashboard, then tried not to sneeze at the cloud of dust he had disturbed.

His dry wit was not lost on Jenny who returned his smile and relaxed against the worn seat cover. Any man who could tolerate Bob with such good humor couldn't be all bad.

They split an order of deluxe nachos that were piled high with meat, refried beans, guacamole, and sour cream at a small Mexican restaurant that Jenny recommended and sipped icy margaritas as they talked.

"So what type of facility are you building here in Corpus?" she asked.

"We're building a sort of combination laboratory and sea animal exhibition. There will be several large tanks where the water temperature can be regulated and changed for our experiments as well as smaller display tanks that will show the fish in their natural environment. One of the things we want to study is whether or not white whales can adapt to warm water conditions."

"I don't believe I've ever heard of a white whale before. They must not get this far south very often."

"No, they stay in the Arctic bays, sometimes ranging north of the Soviet Union, but they rarely migrate any farther south than Canada. They're about twice as big as dolphins, but without the dorsal fin. Their heads are shaped sort of like a porpoise's, but their bodies are built like snow white thermos bottles. What we want to find out is if their blubber layer, which is usually about three inches thick, will shrink as they grow accustomed to slightly warmer water. Because the newborn calves have only a thin layer of fat and do very well in the shallow, warmer parts of the bays, we have reason to believe that these whales could acclimatize themselves. If we could increase their home range, they not only would have more room to roam, but would be easier to protect in the friendly seas of the United States territorial water."

"And the public will be able to view the whales after this place is built?" Jenny asked, as she put a bite of cheese enchilada in her mouth.

"Yes, and besides the white whales, Sea-Free will have a pair of orcas, better known as killer whales, some dolphins, seals, sea lions, and a viewing tank holding rays and sharks."

"It sounds like a big project." Jenny studied her chalupa with an inordinate amount of concentration as she added, "How long do you figure it will take to build?"

"Overall, probably about a year, but I'll be through with my part of Phase I by the end of July."

So he would only be here for a couple of months more. Jenny swallowed a sigh. Again she reminded herself that she must not get too attached to him because he would soon be sailing away. And she must not let him see how disappointed she was or he might get the wrong impression. "Where will you go from here? Do you already have your next job lined up?"

"I believe Pete and I will be doing some work at a couple of resorts in the Caribbean that should, if we time it right, take us most of the winter. And after that, who knows? You mentioned that you're a John Denver fan. Well, so are Pete and I. We even named our sailboat after one of his songs, 'The Eagle and The Hawk.' In our partnership, I am the eagle and I approach our projects with an overall, into the future view, while Pete is the hawk who has blood on his feathers. He's the businessman and does all of our bidding and contract negotiations. So I don't usually keep up with our schedule and he doesn't fool with the actual work on the project."

"I was wondering where Pete fit into this arrangement. He seems like a real nice guy."

"He is, but not as nice as I am," Garrett hurriedly reassured her, flashing her an impudent grin. "Pete and I were roommates at college and after graduation, we begged and borrowed enough money to buy a Sabre 332 sailboat. We are planning on sailing around the world, but first we have to make enough money to pay off the boat and get a little nest egg. So we decided to enter into a partnership and do freelance consulting on anything that has to do with marine biology, such as subsidence, species control and protection, and seawater aquariums like the one we're building here."

He paused and stared over her shoulder, through the window and into the blankness of the night. There was no moon out there to relieve the darkness and it was impossible to tell where the inky water of the bay met the velvet black sky. But instinctively, Garrett knew the direction toward the open sea. It beckoned him with a silent siren's song and had waited patiently for the last seven years while he and Pete worked and saved for their trip.

It wouldn't be long now. After this job and the ones this winter, they would have more than enough money to pay off all their loans and provide them with a comfortable security blanket. Then they could set sail for a leisurely tour of the most exotic ports and the most attractive women in the world.

Garrett's gaze shifted from the future back to the present as he watched Jenny finish off her large Mexican dinner with the gusto of a lumberjack. Intriguing, beautiful, and perplexing, she attracted him in more than just a physical way. She was like a puzzle whose colorful pieces were scattered across a table-top. He would hate to leave until he had put all the pieces together and figured out what it was that made her so appealing. More than likely he would be disappointed when he saw the whole picture. He always had been before with other ladies he had met. It shouldn't take long before he tired of staying in one spot, even with Jenny here to amuse him. Then he could set sail for the adventure of the high seas . . . satisfied that he was leaving behind nothing or no one of any importance.

Jenny looked up and caught him studying her. A hesitant smile parted her lips and the tip of her tongue peeked out to lick off the foamy residue of her drink. She hadn't meant it to be a sensual gesture, but it affected Garrett as if she had been licking the margarita's salt from his own lips instead of hers. Again the heat of desire rushed through his body and his heart danced a calypso in his chest. He had never before met a woman he minded leaving behind.

But Jenny was different.

FOUR

"I don't know how you managed it, but I seem to be doing all the talking this evening," he retorted as the realization suddenly struck him. He couldn't remember a time when he had been more chatty than his date. And now, even after spending several hours with Jenny, he knew little more about her than he had yesterday. "Now it's your turn to tell me everything about yourself," he continued.

The waitress had already picked up their plates, so he put his elbows on the table and, resting his chin on his folded hands, settled his attention on her expressive face.

Jenny tilted her head sideways and lifted one shoulder in a shrug. "There's not much to tell, actually. By most people's standards, I've lived a pretty boring life, especially the last few years since I moved back to Rockport."

"You can start by telling me how you can afford to feed all those hungry mouths. I don't imagine oats and whatever else you have to buy for them is cheap and I also can't believe your salary from the Department of Parks and Wildlife is enough to cover it. Are you secretly an heiress . . . or a bank robber?"

"Neither," she chuckled. "I wasn't lucky enough for the first and I'm not insane enough for the second, although there are several people who say I've done some pretty crazy things lately."

"Now we're getting to the interesting part." Garrett's golden brown eyebrows lifted expectantly as he flashed her another of his rakishly crooked grins. "Does being 'crazy' have anything to do with the *real* reason you're called the Wild Woman?"

"Sort of," she responded, her gold-flecked hazel eyes twinkling devilishly. "But I think you're still going to be disappointed with the truth."

"I can't believe that anything about you could disappoint me," he commented with unexpected sincerity.

"Okay then, I'll tell you the whole boring story. But if you yawn, even once, I won't say another word for the rest of the evening."

He pressed his lips together as if to seal them shut and motioned for her to continue.

Taking a deep breath she began. "Actually, this whole part of my life has been something of an accident. I grew up in Corpus, and even though you could hardly call it a big city, I still preferred being out in the open where there weren't people living ten feet on either side of you. I would spend a lot of my spare time at my grandparents' farm, where they raised cattle and goats, and operated a dairy. I used to help them with the milking, the babies, the farming, and even, much less enthusiastically, the butchering. When you raise farm animals, you learn not to make pets of them, because their sole purpose in life is to provide either food or income. I think that background has helped me with my own animals, even though I'd never dream of eating one of them.

"Anyway, I knew since I was just a little kid that I wanted to be a veterinarian. I got my degree at Texas A&M and set up practice in Houston because I had heard that was where I could make the most money. But after a year of treating poodles with allergies and parrots with laryngitis, I decided that putting up with urban hypochondriacs was not what I wanted out of life.

"Sure, I was making more money than I knew what to do with, but my practice wasn't challenging me. I lived in a huge, perfect house in the Woodlands, I rubbed elbows with high society at all the appropriate charities, but I was having problems with my personal life. My time was so regimented that I couldn't breathe. I was spending four hours a day on the freeways in bumper-to-bumper traffic getting back and forth to my office near the fashionable and exclusive Galleria. I didn't have time to do any of the things I enjoyed most . . . riding and showing horses, walking along the beach, reading romance books, and eating cherries in the summertime. I was miserable.

"So I gave it all up and moved back here. My grandparents had died within a couple months of each other and left me their place. It's really too small to be called a ranch, but I like to think of it as one. I moved in and spent a few months unwinding and trying to decide where I should go from there. One day a friend of mine who works for the Wildlife Department stopped by with a fawn that had been hit by a car. I nursed him back to health and we let him go, but by then that same friend had dropped off an orphaned litter of coyote puppies, a few wounded birds, and an armadillo he had confiscated from a bar where the patrons would get the poor creature drunk and jolt it with an electrical prod to make it win armadillo races.

"I enjoyed working with the wild animals and seemed to have a knack with them, so he sponsored me for a special permit through the state. As you can imagine, after that, everyone for miles around started bringing me injured or orphaned animals, and that's where I got my less than notorious nickname. But what started out as a hobby was suddenly getting very expensive. At first, the Wildlife Department paid me a flat fee for my veterinary services and food, but since the number of animals fluctuates month by month, sometimes it didn't even cover my costs. Even after they went to an expense report payment, I wasn't making enough money to live on and still keep the ranch open. But I was, for the first time, really enjoying my life.

"By chance, I happened to go to a horse show in Corpus and was captivated by the miniature horses that were there. At that time, they weren't being judged but were being shown as an exhibit. They didn't have a class in the competition because there were so few of them. I've always loved horses, and even though they're very expensive to raise, it was clear to me that one day soon there would be a major market for those little animals. And I wanted to get in on the ground floor. Was that a yawn?" she asked suspiciously.

"No, honestly it wasn't. It was just a hiccup," he denied emphatically and took a drink of water to confirm his statement. "You have my full attention. Please go on."

She peered at him doubtfully, but his enthusiastic nod encouraged her to keep talking. By nature, Jenny was extroverted and out-going about everything but her personal life. Her grandparents had taught her to try to solve her own problems and take care of herself. She had forgotten that for a while when she moved away, but she was back home now, on her own, and happy with things the way they were.

Her gaze rested on the man sitting across from her. His thick straight wheat colored hair looked even paler in the soft artificial lights of the restaurant and the snowy white of his pullover shirt made his tan seem even darker. The interest and gentle warmth of his incredibly blue eyes touched her heart as it hadn't been touched by a human in a very long time. It was nice to be out on a real date with a man to whom she felt such a strong attraction. He was gorgeous and just being with him made her feel pretty and desirable. The magnetic pull of his charm was undeniable, but it served as an unwelcome reminder that her life was not as complete and perfect as she had thought. If she wasn't careful, she might actually miss this guy when he was gone.

"So I went to a couple of convents to get some advice," she began again, only to be interrupted by his puzzled exclamation.

"You're not a nun, are you? God, please tell me it isn't true."

"Of course, I'm not a nun, even though lately I've been living like one," she said with a wry snort. "I don't have nearly enough dedication or discipline to live in a convent. Besides, I'm not Catholic and I look terrible in black."

Garrett gave a long exaggerated sigh of relief as he pretended to wipe sweat off his brow. "You had me worried there for a minute."

"Afraid you're wasting your time?" she teased.

"No, just worried that I might get struck by a bolt of lightning because I have no intention of letting anything stand in the way of getting to know you much better." Although there was a hint of humor in his voice, the directness of his gaze told her he wasn't joking. Reaching across the table, he laced his fingers into hers, creating a tangible bond of intimacy between them.

Jenny's stomach tightened and her heart somersaulted before settling back down to the double-time patter it seemed to have adopted since she had first met Garrett. "Are you always this shy?" she managed to ask, her tongue firmly planted in her cheek.

"Only with wild women."

"And how many wild women have you met?"

"Not enough."

"I'll bet."

"No, wait. I don't want you to get the wrong impression. I don't want you to think I'm some sort of high-seas playboy." He squeezed her fingers and lifted her hand to his lips, slowly and sensually planting a tender kiss on each of her fingertips. "This has been one of the nicest evenings I've spent in a long time and I don't want it to end with a misunderstanding."

"Oh no," Jenny exclaimed, straightening abruptly in her chair. With a twist of her arm that Garrett still held captive, she scanned her watch and repeated, "Oh no. Garrett, I'm sorry, but I've got to go. I didn't realize it was so late."

"Late? It's only nine o'clock," he protested. "Too early for bed . . . or do you have a late date?"

Jenny rolled her eyes at that suggestion, picked up her purse, and stood up. "Nothing so romantic as that, I'm afraid. I've just got to drive into Corpus and do a little special grocery shopping."

"Grocery shopping?" he echoed as he picked up the check and followed her to the exit.

"I told you I lived a boring life."

As they drove back to her ranch, Garrett regretfully had to keep both hands on the wheel to hold the roving vehicle on the black-topped highway. "Do you need any help?"

"Help with my groceries?" she asked, passing him a mischievous grin. "You don't know what you're getting yourself into."

Dragging his attention away from his driving long enough to give her a puzzled look, he said, a little defensively, "I've been grocery shopping before. I don't claim to be a good cook, but I'm not one of those helpless males who can't wash his own socks or buy his own bacon."

"Somehow I can't visualize you clipping coupons or comparison pricing," she chuckled. "But if you want to go with me, I have no objections. Just let me warn you ahead of time that this is like no other grocery shopping you've ever done. You might be sorry you wore white tonight. That's why I'm stopping at the house to change clothes."

Garrett didn't have a clue what she was talking about, but he was game for a new adventure. He steered Bob into the driveway and pulled to a stop next to her house.

It was late and the chickens and goose had already roosted, so only the dog and a few cats greeted them as they walked to the back door. Inside, however, three spitting bundles of fur immediately attached themselves to their legs. Jenny looked down at the trail of white marks left on her tanned skin by a set of tiny claws.

"Now you know why I don't bother with stockings. I'd be spending more on them than on all my other clothes combined," she remarked, tossing her purse on the table and crossing the room.

Garrett was too busy admiring her long, shapely limbs to comment. The thought that they were bare beneath her skirt was incredibly exciting to him, even though the shorts she had worn earlier had left little to his imagination. It seemed like every time she changed her clothes, she appealed to a different facet of his being, until they were combining into an almost uncomfortable desire for all of her . . . not just her body, but *all* of her.

He was almost relieved when she returned to the room a few minutes later and her legs were completely covered by a pair of form-fitting blue jeans and a loose chambray shirt disguising much of the rest of her feminine curves.

"Let's go," she said as she pulled her hair back into a ponytail and secured it with an elastic band. "We've got about a dozen stops to make after we get to Corpus and I don't want to keep you out too late."

Soon they were bouncing along the dark highway heading toward Corpus Christi. As Garrett's teeth jarred together after a particularly rough dip in the road, he ventured to ask, "I don't mean to hurt ol' Bob's feelings, but when is the last time he had a new set of shocks?"

"You mean shock absorbers? I have no idea. I'm afraid automobile maintenance is my weak point. I can shoe a horse, but I have trouble changing a spark plug," she admitted, almost apologetically.

"I can't believe it! At last, I've found something that you're not good at doing," he crowed.

"Well, don't sound so smug. I think, under the circumstances, that I've managed quite nicely."

"Now don't get all defensive. I didn't mean to hurt your feelings. It's just that you have no idea how upsetting it is to meet someone who seems to have her life totally in control. I was beginning to believe you didn't need anyone for anything."

Jenny turned her head away from him so he couldn't read her expression in the dim light from the dashboard. All she could distinguish in the night-camouflaged landscape was the endless row of fence posts that appeared to be marching rapidly by. She didn't want him to see the loneliness in her eyes or discover that he had stumbled upon a major vulnerability. Again, the pep talk she had been giving herself for the last six years pumped through her brain, but its effects seemed to be diminishing. There was a possibility that she did need someone to make her life complete, but it just couldn't be Garrett. Why did he, of all the men in the world, have to stir all these long-dormant feelings into a heated inferno? It just wasn't fair. Why was her choice of men always doomed to failure?

"Jenny? Did I say something wrong?"

"No, of course not," she denied, shaking off the moodiness that had been brought on by her thoughts. "I was just thinking about everything I've learned over the last few years. My priorities had to be rearranged so the things that needed my attention most got it first. I guess I've pushed everything that doesn't breathe and eat, such as fixing up Bob and painting my house, into the background until I have time to deal with them."

"When do you take time just for yourself? What do you do for fun?"

"You make it sound like I'm sacrificing myself to a cause or something. It's not that way at all. I *really* like the animals and the ranch. I enjoy not waking up to the buzz of an alarm clock or having to go to cocktail parties. I can sleep as late as my roosters will allow and invite whomever or whatever I want into my living room to watch 'Mr. Ed' reruns. I admit that sometimes I miss being involved in a steady relationship, but I haven't found anyone who would like to share my lifestyle and can understand why I could never again give it up."

Garrett nodded. He understood. He shared her love of animals and dislike of a predictable, sedate lifestyle. But she was grounded to the land and he was in love with the freedom of the seas. She enjoyed the fragrance of fresh hay and horses, while he savored the salty freshness of the air that blew across the water and filled the stiff blue and white sails of his boat, pushing him away from the shoreline. As far as he could see, he and Jenny had no mediate ground, no basis for trying to make something more of this budding attraction they felt for each other.

Why was he wasting his time with her then? Because she fascinated him more than any one else and because he liked her . . . a lot. Not to mention the fact that she affected his libido like it hadn't been affected lately. They might not have a future together, but as long as they both were aware of that, there was no reason why they couldn't have one heck of a present while he was working here.

"You never did finish your life story," he reminded her, still wanting to know everything there was to know about her. "Why did you visit those convents if you weren't planning on becoming a nun or making a confession about your *wild* life?"

"My *wild*life had everything to do with it," she answered, relieved that the conversation was returning to a less threatening subject. "There are two convents in Texas where the nuns raise miniature horses, so I went to them for advice. I figured if you couldn't trust a nun to tell you the truth, then who could you trust? They showed me their stock and told me the incredible prices they were getting for some of their horses. Even if I hadn't already fallen in love with the animals themselves, I would have been attracted by the profit margin. Most of them sell for around twenty-five hundred each, but a really fine stallion sold for thirty thousand and several others have gone for between ten and seventeen thousand. The price depends on their size and confirmation.

"It seemed to be the answer to my money problems. Not only were they sweet and intelligent, but they were easy to manage, cheap to feed, and would fit into the environment of the ranch. So I sold my car, cashed in my last C.D., and jumped off the deep end. I started with five mares and two stallions and in the last three years my herd has grown to fourteen with the ones I have sold bringing in over a hundred thousand dollars.''

"And that's not chicken feed," Garrett interrupted.

"Actually, it is, because most of the money has gone back into the ranch, but it's worth it.'' They had crossed the bridge over Corpus Christi Bay and were driving downtown. "Turn right at the next traffic light," she told him, then pointed out the grocery store a few blocks down. "Drive around to the back and park next to those boxes.''

"But I see a space right in front of the doors," he protested.

"This type of shopping has to be done from behind the store," she explained.

He gave her a strange look, but obediently parked the truck where she had indicated. Jenny hopped out and went to a pair of heavy metal doors that had been propped open. Garrett sat in the truck, watching as Jenny strode inside as if she belonged there. A couple of minutes later, she reappeared, her arms loaded with a large cardboard box, filled to overflowing with some sort of green leafy vegetable.

Garrett pushed open Bob's door and vaulted out, hurrying to her side to offer his help. "Here, let me take that. It looks heavy.''

"No, I can handle this one. This is just spinach leaves and it's not as heavy as it looks. But there's a box of carrots inside the door that is very heavy. You can get that one, if you don't mind.''

They passed each other on their repeated trips from the storeroom to the truck until a half dozen boxes had been loaded.

"Thanks. I'll see you Monday night . . . same time, same place," Jenny called to the store manager as she made her final trip to the truck.

"I'll be out some day next week to pick out a kitten for my daughter's birthday," the manager called back, before pulling the heavy doors shut.

"So this is how you grocery shop," Garrett remarked as they headed for their next store. "Don't tell me you eat this stuff."

"Of course not. These are scraps or over-ripe vegetables that are still edible, but not attractive enough for the customers. My horses don't care if the carrots are a little withered and the rabbits don't mind eating collard greens that have brown edges. No matter what kind of vegetable they give me, at least one of my animals will eat it. It saves me a lot of money and is very good for them. About the only thing I don't bother with is iceberg lettuce because it has almost no nutritional value. The greener the leaf, the better it is for for man and beast both."

"Thank you, Professor Grant," he teased, earning himself an elbow in the ribs.

For the next two hours they drove all over the city, stopping at several other stores until the back of the truck was loaded as high as safely possible. After throwing the tarp over the boxes and tying it down to the wooden slats that were attached to the top of the truck's sides, Garrett and Jenny headed back toward the ranch.

They were only a few miles away from Rockport when Garrett noticed the flashing red and blue lights of a highway patrol car reflecting in his side mirrors.

"Damn," he muttered, automatically glancing at the speedometer. "Hey, we're not even going forty miles an hour. What's the speed limit on this road?"

"Fifty-five, I think, but I usually don't pay much attention to speed limit signs. Bob won't go over forty-five, and everyone usually passes us as if we were standing still."

"Maybe he's after that red Trans Am that passed us a few minutes ago," Garrett noted hopefully as he steered Bob off the road and waited for the patrol car to pass.

It didn't. Instead, it pulled in behind them and a uniformed officer got out of the car and walked toward them.

"Maybe we didn't tie the tarp down good enough," Garrett continued to fret. "I don't know why police cars make me so nervous, but they do . . . even when I know I haven't done anything wrong."

"I think they affect everyone like that. But if you know you weren't violating a law, then stand up for your rights."

"No, I just want to get this over with as quickly and painlessly as possible," he replied, rolling down the window and getting his wallet out of his pocket.

The officer flashed his light in the window and peered in at them. But before he could speak, Jenny spoke in an obviously disrespectful voice, "What's the matter, officer? Couldn't you catch any of the other cars, so you decided to pick on us?"

"*Jenny* . . ." Garrett warned in a low voice.

But she couldn't be silenced. "Haven't you filled

your quota of tickets yet for this evening? Or do you want to check under our tarp to see if we're carrying a load of drugs or illegal aliens?''

"*Jenny!*" Garrett practically bellowed as his rounded blue eyes gave her a horror-stricken stare. "Don't joke with the policeman, Jennifer. He's an officer of the law, just doing his duty."

"In that case, dő you take bribes, officer?" she continued with a sweet smile.

Garrett collapsed limply against the seat, positive they would both be arrested at any minute and thrown into jail. What had gotten into her? Why had she picked this moment to stand up for her rights?

"All right, out of the car, both of you," the officer demanded.

Jenny shrugged and opened her door as Garrett exited from his door, his hands lifted in the air. Spreading his legs, he leaned forward against the hood, expecting to be searched as he had seen them do on the cop shows on television.

Jenny walked around the truck and stopped when she was directly in front of the officer, boldly facing him.

"It's a rotten shame when I have to use my authority to chase you down, just so I can see you again," the officer laughed, reaching out and pulling Jenny into a big bear hug. "Where have you been keeping yourself lately, Jen? It's been weeks."

"That's no excuse, Jeff. You know where I live. You can come out to see me just as easily as I can go see you," she retorted, returning his hug.

"Hey, what's going on here?" Garrett asked, peering over his shoulder at them. When he saw them embracing, he straightened, and turned around to stare. "Jenny, remember me? Who is this guy?"

Jeff let Jenny go and looked over at Garrett as if he were seeing him for the first time. "Who is this guy?" he echoed, turning the tables on Garrett.

"This is Garrett Reid, a marine biologist who's helping design the Sea-Free facility near Corpus. And, Garrett, this is Jeff Grant, my brother and my favorite highway patrol officer." Jenny reached out and took Garrett's hand, drawing him closer to her as she made the introductions.

"It's pretty late to be out," Jeff commented with a pointed glance at his watch.

"Garrett and I have been hitting the grocery stores for hand outs tonight and were on our way back to the ranch. Besides, I'm twenty-eight years old and don't have to check in with you any more when I stay out late. What are you going to do, report me to Mom?"

"Of course, I am. You know how excited she'll be when I tell her you were on a date and that you even let him drive Bob," Jeff teased, then punched Garrett with his elbow. "You have no idea what an honor it is for her to let you drive that stupid old truck. I can remember begging to borrow it, but she told me it was temperamental and would only respond to her."

"Jeff . . ." This time it was Jenny's turn to threaten him to silence. "We've got to be going. These vegetables need to be refrigerated as soon as possible and it's getting late."

"Okay, but I have something for you in the car."
As Jeff returned to the patrol car, Garrett confronted
Jenny with a gruff, but relieved growl.

"You little minx. You let me think he was going
to arrest us, when all the time you knew it was just
your brother."

"I'm sorry," she said, but the twinkle in her eyes
told him that was only partially true. "I didn't mean
to upset you, it's just that when I saw it was Jeff, I
couldn't resist. You should have seen your face when
I offered him a bribe. It was hilarious."

"I should . . ." he hesitated, trying to think of an
appropriate punishment. He gripped her arms and
pulled her roughly against him. "I should spank you,
but all I can think about is kissing that smile off your
pretty little face."

"Promises, promises," she taunted with uncharacteristic coquetry, and didn't move away as he leaned
toward her.

His lips pressed against hers, hard at first, but
quickly softening into a sensuous embrace. For a few
seconds, he forgot that they were standing next to a
highway in the middle of the night. All he could
think of was the woman in his arms.

"Boy, Mother's going to love this," Jeff exclaimed
as he returned. "She was beginning to think you'd
never give her any grandchildren."

Garrett and Jenny exchanged private looks, filled
with questions and desires. They were both feeling
the same things, but neither knew what should be
done about it. The obvious answer would be to take

what pleasure they could from the moment and try not to think about the future. But would either of them be satisfied with that?

"I think you'd be getting Mother's hopes up for nothing, Jeff," Jenny stated simply, unable to hide the wistful smile that played at the corners of her mouth, threatening to pull them down, rather than up. Forcing her attention away from Garrett's handsome face, she walked over to Jeff and tried to see what was wrapped in the white towel he was holding.

"What have we got here?" she asked, pushing aside the material until a pair of huge golden eyes stared back at her. "A baby great horned owl," she exclaimed. "Where did you get him?"

"I found him in the road about an hour ago. I think he was hit by a car or something. He was just lying there, dazed. If I hadn't picked him up, he would have been run over for sure. I was going to drop him by your place when I got off my shift, so it's lucky I caught you now. I wasn't sure how I could explain having to share a seat with an owl if I had had to pick someone up and take them in to the station."

Jenny took the bundle from him and said, "I'll take good care of him. We'd better hurry before he gets hysterical. Thanks, Jeff. Tell Mom hi . . . but nothing else."

"Spoil sport," Jeff muttered good-naturedly.

At the ranch, Jenny gave the owl a brief examination and decided he had just been stunned. Nothing was broken and there was no sign of internal injuries, but with a patient that couldn't tell her where it hurt, she could never be certain. Making him as comfortable as possible in a large, outdoor cage, she left him some water, then went to help Garrett unload the truck.

He was almost finished when she joined him, and together, they bagged the vegetables and put them in the large commercial-size refrigerators she had in the barn. It was after one o'clock when they sat, exhausted, on the tailgate of the truck and stared at the pile of empty cardboard boxes they had unloaded.

Garrett flexed his shoulder muscles and yawned. "How often do you do this?"

"Usually twice a week, depending on how many animals I have to feed."

"Twice a week! By yourself?"

"Unless someone happens to drop by and begs to come along," she answered with a tired grin.

"Some sucker, you mean." He yawned again. "I had no idea that this evening would end this way. But you've worn me out. I'm too tired to even think about being romantic."

"I find that hard to believe."

"Well, maybe just one little kiss," he chuckled. "But I promise, I'll make it up to you tomorrow night. Maybe we could go see a movie or something."

Jenny shivered as a tingle of anticipation, mixed with a healthy dose of apprehension streaked through her body. So he planned on seeing her again tomorrow night. The idea did not displease her, even though she would have to rearrange some plans she had already made. She wouldn't have dreamed of telling Garrett that it wasn't convenient; she liked him enough that she would willingly adjust her schedule for the next few weeks so that she could be with him. She knew that this decision was neither wise nor realistic, but she couldn't force her mouth to tell him to leave. Certainly not with the same lips that had melted beneath his and, even now, could still taste the delightful flavor of his kiss.

The truth was that she liked being around him, hearing his laughter and sharing intelligent conversations. Unfortunately though, the more she was with him, the more she would feel the loss when he was gone. If she wasn't careful, she might be so foolish as to fall in love with him.

Surely she wouldn't do something that stupid. She knew better than to fall in love with a wild thing.

FIVE

It wasn't a rooster's crow that woke Jenny the next morning. At first she tried to ignore the offending noise, but the hum of her fan did little to muffle the loud sputtering of a diesel engine that poured into her open windows. For a few moments, she nestled deeper into her pillow, suspended between sleep and total wakefulness. Although she knew it was time to get up, a part of her clung to the warmth and happiness of the dream that had been so abruptly interrupted. She couldn't remember exactly what the dream had been about, but just that it had been pleasant and she hadn't wanted it to end.

As reality gradually penetrated her consciousness, thoughts of last night replaced the lingering remnants of the dream. She had had such a nice time with

Garrett. She couldn't remember the last time she had
laughed so much or had such fun.

The motor coughed to life again and Jenny sat up.
Pushing her tangled hair back from her forehead, she
swung her legs over the side of the bed and walked to
the window. She had no idea what could be making
such a racket. Her view from the window offered no
visible explanation, so she hurriedly dressed and went
outside, following the noise to the back of the garage.

"What on earth are you doing?" she asked as she
was met with the sight of Rusty peering into the open
engine of her grandfather's dilapidated old tractor.
She couldn't remember the last time she had heard
that engine working, and she had forgotten just how
loud it was.

Rusty glanced over his shoulder and flashed her a
tentative grin. "Just thought I'd see if I could get this
baby going. It doesn't look like she's had much
attention lately. Everything's dirty and corroded."
The grease smudges on his face and arms provided
proof to his statement.

"It broke down a few years before Grandpa died,"
Jenny confirmed. "Since I couldn't afford to have it
fixed and wasn't planning to cultivate any of the
fields, I haven't touched it. Besides, I didn't know if
it would be worth putting any money into an antique
like that."

"Are you kidding?" The boy looked at the faded
tractor with obvious affection. "They don't make
equipment like they used to. These old engines should

last forever . . . that is, if they have someone to take care of them. It just so happens diesels are my specialty. I could have this tractor in tiptop shape in no time.''

Jenny cast a doubtful glance at the rusted machine.

''You know the field next to the windmill?'' he continued. ''It looks like it was used for farming at one time. Someone has already cleared the rocks and leveled it off. The mesquite and prickly pear are trying to take over again, but with a little work, we could have that field planted in a week and have at least one cutting of hay before fall . . . maybe two if we get the right amount of rain.''

It dawned on Jenny that Rusty was including himself in the future of the ranch. He might not even be aware of it, but whether it was consciously or subconsciously, he was trying to convince her she needed him and that the ranch would be better off as a result of his efforts. Already, he had been here longer than she had planned. But he had proven to be helpful with whatever chores she had given him. And, more importantly, she still hadn't been able to dig up a clue about his background. It was obvious he didn't want to return to wherever it was he had come from which appealed to her protective instincts. And right now he needed to feel like he belonged somewhere, even if it was temporary.

''Yes, I think that would be a good idea. If we could put up a few dozen bales of hay, it would save some money this winter,'' she agreed, offering him encouragement. "I don't have much extra money for parts, but if you think you can get this tractor going, then let's do it."

Almost visibly she could see his self-confidence grow in proportion to the responsibility she had just entrusted him with. "Yes, ma'am. I'll have her purring like a pussy cat in no time." He gestured toward the garage where he had sorted and stored boxes of parts. "I should be able to find whatever I need right in here. It looks like your granddad never threw anything away and he must have kept the parts from other tractors. I could almost build another whole tractor from what's in those boxes."

"I'd settle for just one that works," Jenny replied with a wry chuckle. "I'll call you when breakfast is ready."

Eagerly he returned to work, climbing up to stand on the hard rubber wheel so he could reach inside the engine. He seemed to be a good kid, trying hard to overcome a bad situation and improve his life.

Jenny went to the barn and checked the animals. They were still contentedly munching on their own breakfasts, reassuring her that Rusty had done the morning chores before digging into his new project. After returning to the house, she fed the baby bobcats before stirring together some buttermilk biscuits. While she fried a few strips of bacon and a couple of eggs for Rusty, she couldn't help but wonder where he had come from and why he had left. He still hadn't volunteered any information.

After the first few days, she had decided to take Jeff into her confidence and had him run Rusty's name and description through the police computer. When no reports of a missing boy even remotely matched, Jenny had become even more curious and even more determined to offer this human "stray" a shelter where he could weather his personal storm.

The stiff wind off the bay tugged at his clothes and threatened to rip the blueprints out of his hands. Garrett struggled to hold them flat, but the corners kept curling in until he finally gave up, twisted the heavy paper into a long roll and tucked it under his arm. He had been trying to visualize the proposed structure as it would look when built on the bare stretch of land in front of him. Huge bulldozers and draglines worked to redesign the topography, flattening the dunes, building up the sand where the structure's foundations would be and digging deep holes where the tanks would be. Garrett knew that someday it would be a modern laboratory for the study and viewing of sea animals, but right now everything looked like a disaster had struck. But there was more organization to the scene than appeared at first glance.

The job was coming along well. The weather was cooperating and the workmen were obviously skilled. With any luck, his part of the project would be finished soon and he could be on his way.

Garrett realized he was frowning. Somehow the thought of leaving this area soon was not as appealing as it should have been. His gaze lifted to the open water whose surface was being kicked into ruffles by the wind, but not quite white-capping. Seagulls dipped and dove into the sparkling green liquid, sometimes coming up with a protesting fish, and sometimes coming up with something disappointing like an empty shell or a piece of paper.

He wasn't sure what it was—perhaps the antics of the birds or maybe the familiar green color of the water—but Garrett was reminded of the real reason he wasn't anxious to leave. Jennifer Grant was proving to be a more interesting project than Sea-Free.

"What planet are you on?"

The unexpected voice cut into Garrett's thoughts and he looked down, startled to see Pete sitting in a car only a few feet away.

"I've been yelling at you for the last five minutes," Pete complained jokingly. "Didn't you hear me?"

Not only hadn't he heard his friend calling, but he hadn't even heard the car drive up. "No, I guess the machinery and the wind were too loud," Garrett explained as he walked closer.

"Yeah, sure," Pete replied, totally unconvinced. "You wouldn't have been thinking about a certain lady who likes to swim fully dressed and looks better in wet jeans than almost anyone I know, would you?"

Garrett knew there was no reason to deny it and accepted Pete's teasing with a smile. "I've seen women in bikinis that didn't look as sexy as Jenny did,'' he admitted. ''And you should have seen her last night . . . well, maybe it was a good thing you didn't. The competition for her time and attention is already tough enough.''

One of Pete's dark brown eyebrows lifted as he commented, ''You're making all the sounds of a man who is falling in love.''

''That's crazy,'' Garrett snorted. ''I've only seen her twice and neither time could be described as normal. She's merely a nice, friendly woman in a strange city.''

''Just keep thinking about all those gorgeous babes waiting for us in the Caribbean. I'll bet they're nice and friendly, too.''

Garrett knew when that thought didn't excite him, he was in trouble.

''What sounds good for lunch?'' Pete asked.

The rest of the day Garrett tried to concentrate on the job. But time and again an image of Jenny or a memory of last night would somehow filter into his thoughts.

Hours later when he was straddling the small motorcycle and zipping down the road heading for her house he couldn't help but wonder what this evening had in store. Would they share a quiet dinner and see a movie as planned or would they be delivering a litter of raccoons or rescuing an orphaned opossum from a raging river? Or would they actually have a few moments alone so he could take her in his arms and . . . His blood quickened at the possibilities and he tried to urge more speed out of the not overly powerful engine beneath him.

When he arrived at her ranch and Bob was missing from the driveway, he tried not to be too disappointed. Perhaps the decrepit truck was in the shop or had died completely. Garrett parked his motorcycle next to the barn and, after passing an intense inspection by Rags and Mother, he opened the gate and walked across the yard to the back door. His knock roused hungry growls from inside, but still there was no sign of Jenny.

He glanced at his watch and saw that he was almost a half hour early, so he sat on the step and tried to wait patiently. Forty-five minutes later, he wasn't sure whether he was more concerned that she had apparently forgotten their date or that she might be stranded somewhere. Restlessly, Garrett stood up and tried to decide whether to wait here or try to find her. It didn't help that he had no idea which direction she might have gone or when.

The sound of a tractor sputtering to life behind the garage caught his attention and he sighed with a mixture of relief and aggravation. So she was involved in another handyman project and didn't realize what time it was. He wasn't accustomed to being treated with such disregard, but he was willing to listen to her excuses.

Garrett rounded the corner of the garage, the words of a gentle reprimand already formulating in his mind. But before he could speak he was halted by the sight of a young man sitting on the seat of the noisy machine. Another brother?

When the boy saw Garrett, it was difficult to say who was more surprised. For a full minute they shared a silent stare, each measuring the other and trying to decide who should speak first. It was Garrett who finally voiced the question they both wanted to ask.

"Who are you?"

The boy shifted uncomfortably and began wiping his oily hands on a rag with studied intensity. "A friend," he finally muttered, then lifted his gaze to Garrett and countered with an equally wary, "Who are you?"

"A friend," Garrett echoed, amused at the ferocity of the young man's expression and yet curious how this male fit into her life. But sensing that this was not the time for a confrontation, even if the boy would fill him in on the details which Garrett doubted, he continued the conversation with the hope that at least this boy might know where Jenny was. "Jenny and I were supposed to have a date this evening, but it looks like she stood me up."

The boy frowned. "You mean she hasn't come back yet? What time is it?"

Garrett looked at his watch again and answered. "Almost six thirty. Where did she go?"

"I'm not sure, but I don't think she planned on being gone this long. Right after lunch she got a phone call. I don't know who it was or what it was about, but she dropped everything and went rushing out of here like she was in a huge hurry about something. I guess I got busy working on this tractor and didn't realize it was so late." The boy's appraising gaze swept Garrett's body from the tip of his Reeboks to the top of his golden blond head. For another moment he hesitated as if considering whether or not Garrett could be trusted, then made a decision to continue, volunteering further information. "She did remember your date because she mentioned it at lunch. She seemed pretty excited about it, so I don't think she's late on purpose."

Garrett felt a surge of pleasure at the thought Jenny was looking forward to this evening as much as he was, but then the worry about what might have delayed her took over.

"Did you see which way she headed when she left?" he asked. "Maybe that old truck of hers broke down and she had to hitch a ride to a service station."

"No, I was back here and didn't see which way she went. She just said there was an emergency and she wouldn't be gone long."

They were both quiet as they considered the possibilities and hoped their worst fears would be ungrounded.

"Do you think she would mind if we went into the house? Maybe she wrote something down that would give us a clue," Garrett suggested.

"I suppose it would be okay."

"You never did tell me your name," Garrett said, as they walked toward the house.

"Rusty. And you're . . . ?"

"Garrett." He solemnly held his hand out to the younger man. "Nice to meet you, Rusty. Let's hope out mutual friend, Jenny, isn't in trouble somewhere."

Carefully they opened the back door, pushing the kittens back so they could step inside. From the living room they could hear the blare of the television and Garrett led the way toward the sound. Jenny had apparently been in such a hurry that she hadn't taken the time to turn it off. Garrett pushed open the connecting door, intending to block the kittens from escaping into the rest of the house, but the news story on the television screen totally captivated his attention.

"For several hours this afternoon, protestors blocked the entrances of the laboratory, not allowing visiting scientists to enter the building."

The camera showed videotape of a group of people marching in a tight line in front of the doorway, flashing their picket signs toward the camera so the world could see the printed messages. "THERE IS NO EXCUSE FOR TORTURE" and "ANIMALS HAVE FEELINGS, TOO" were the most popular phrases, but some of the signs contained painfully graphic pictures of lab animals being used for experiments.

"Look! There's Jenny!" Rusty exclaimed, pointing at the screen.

Garrett leaned closer and saw that, sure enough, Jenny was right in the thick of things. As he and Rusty watched, a group of the protestors, including Jenny, broke away and stormed the building, going inside. The next scene showed the police leading the protestors back out, and Garrett groaned when he saw the handcuffs clamped around Jenny's arm.

"This doesn't look good for your date," Rusty commented with a muffled chortle.

Garrett passed him an exasperated glance, then looked back at the screen. "I wonder if she has someone to post her bail. Maybe I should go to Corpus and see if I can help."

"Or maybe you could go home," Rusty added bluntly.

This time Garrett turned his full attention to the younger man. What did Jenny mean to Rusty anyway? Whatever it was sure unleashed a protective, almost possessive streak that brought new questions to his mind.

"I like Jenny, too," Garrett responded with a measured calm. "I wouldn't do anything to hurt her."

Rusty snorted his disbelief.

"What have I ever done to make you distrust me?"

"It's not what you've done, but what you're going to do." Rusty thrust his hands as deeply as possible into the pockets of his too-tight, out-grown jeans.

"What has she told you about me?" Garrett was now totally perplexed.

"She hasn't told me anything except that you'll be leaving before the end of the summer, which sounds to me like you're just playing around with her," Rusty explained with surprisingly mature insight.

"What if she falls in love with you? She deserves better than to be a summer fling, you know."

Garrett didn't know how to respond to Rusty's observations. This was the second time today someone had questioned his intentions toward Jenny. Absently he rubbed his hand across his forehead, massaging away the first tinges of a headache. "I barely know Jenny," he finally stated. "This is only our second date and I would hardly call that a guarantee of love or even seduction. And while I'm sure she would appreciate your concern for her welfare, she can certainly take care of herself. She's a big girl."

"Who's a big girl?"

Both men whirled around and stared at the source of the feminine voice behind them. "Jenny!" they exclaimed simultaneously.

"My, my, a stereo greeting." She laughed and walked toward them. "Sorry I'm late. Something came up and . . ."

"You're not in jail," Garrett said, realizing immediately that he had stated the obvious. But he was so surprised—and pleased—to see her that he couldn't think of a single intelligent thing to say.

"Of course not. They wouldn't dare press charges or they would get a ton of bad publicity. This whole thing is their fault anyway. If they hadn't reneged on their promise to sit down and discuss their plans for animal experimentation with the United Action for Animals representatives, we wouldn't have had to picket their lab." Jenny placed her purse on the couch and sat down on a chair whose frayed padded arms showed evidence of an animal's claws.

"Corptech started out as an acceptable laboratory with a minimal use of animals for its medical research," she continued, sitting on the edge of the chair showing she was still charged up over the incident. "But as they expanded, they began using animals for weird, unnecessary experiments. You wouldn't believe the awful things some labs do to live animals, including blinding, burning, poisoning, and even operating on them without anesthesia. This afternoon the local SPCA called me with a report that the executive officers of the company were visiting to inspect the additional labs and to make recommendations that the operations be expanded." Jenny shrugged. "And I just had to be there, to express my disapproval."

"Well, you expressed your disapproval in front of the entire viewing audience because your arrest made the evening news," Garrett informed her.

She clapped her hands, then twined her fingers together in a gesture of triumph. "That's terrific! I saw the cameras, but I was afraid they wouldn't think saving a few thousand animal lives would be as important as showing the result of a bike race in the Rockies or something else insignificant. Maybe if those executives get a dose of bad publicity, they'll reconsider their plans."

Rusty cast a glance from Jenny to Garrett, then back to Jenny, as if trying to decide whether or not it was wise to leave the two of them alone. Apparently feeling a little uncomfortable, he said, "I guess I'd better get to the evening chores. I'm glad you're not going to spend the night in the slammer."

"The slammer?" Jenny repeated with a laugh. "I think you've been watching too many old movies. Do you think you can handle feeding the animals alone tonight? I need to take a bath and get dressed."

"No problem. I can take care of everything," he assured her as he straightened to his full height and threw back his shoulders. "And don't worry about my dinner. I can make sandwiches from the leftover ham."

Jenny smiled affectionately at him as he turned and walked out of the room. "Isn't he a nice kid? He's been a big help to me around here."

"Better than a guard dog," Garrett muttered under his breath. "Or even a guard goose." He had just moved to the couch and sat down when he noticed a tiny pink nose and white whiskers poking out from under the flap of her purse. When a furry head, two beady red eyes, and a pair of round pink ears became visible, Garrett reached down and let the animal scurry onto his hand. "I must admit that you're the first woman I've ever dated who had a mouse in her purse. I'm sure there's a perfectly logical explanation." He paused and watched the small creature scramble up his arm. "On the other hand, there probably isn't a logical explanation."

Jenny stood up and walked to the hall closet. After digging through a pile of boots and books, she pulled out an aquarium, which she placed on the coffee table. "It's refreshing to know someone who isn't afraid of a little white mouse," she said, taking the animal from him and placing it in the aquarium before securing a mesh screen on the top. "It's amazing how many macho men can't stand to touch anything remotely rodent like."

They watched the small creature explore his new surroundings, its tiny nose twitching. Jenny laughed as she added, "This afternoon the television camera missed the best part of the whole protest demonstration. Apparently a delivery man had just left a box of white mice at the reception desk, and somehow the box got turned over. You wouldn't believe how quickly a room can clear when there are dozens of these little guys running around. You know the cartoons with women standing on chairs and screaming. Well, imagine· that multiplied by twenty or thirty. The men, even some of the scientists who handle mice all the time, were practically knocking the women down to get up on the desks. It was a scene right out of a Laurel and Hardy movie." She laughed out loud at the memory. "I suppose it was then that one of them crawled into my purse and made a break for freedom."

"Rodents aren't my favorite creatures, but I raised my share of them when I was a little boy. None for experiments, I would like to add."

"You won't be too happy to hear what other animals besides the usual dogs, cats, monkeys, goats, and calves they had scheduled for the experiments. When I was inside the building I had a chance to get a quick look around and in the warehouse they had set up a huge tank.'' She paused for dramatic effect, carefully watching his reaction. She knew she would be able to get a fairly accurate character reading by the sincerity and depth of his response. "In it were two dolphins. Goodness knows what sort of torture they have in mind for them, but when I saw the mortality rate of their past projects, I was horrified."

He stood up slowly, the evidence of his fury visible in the sudden sobering of his expression. Jenny hadn't noticed before the hard line of his jaw or the way his nostrils flared ominously. Always before, his features had been tempered by a lively sense of humor and good-natured charm so that Jenny hadn't given him much credit for a serious side.

"What's the address of that lab?" he asked, reaching in his pocket for his keys.

Jenny reached out and grabbed his forearms. Her fingers didn't begin to encompass the surprisingly muscular width of his arms and yet her gentle touch halted him. "There's no need for you to go there tonight. Corptech has been shut down, at least temporarily, by a court order. Today's demonstration was simply a delaying tactic to divert their attention until we have time to process the order. As soon as the Corptech officials declined to press charges, they were presented with a directive to cease and desist all use of animals for experimentation."

She felt him relax beneath her hands. "If you'd like, I'm sure we could get permission for you to examine the dolphins tomorrow or the next day," she suggested.

He took a deep, steadying breath. "Yes, I think that would be a good idea. You might need some expert witnesses when this gets to court."

Jenny nodded her agreement.

"Now if you're still interested in going out with me tonight, we'd better get moving." Garrett's smile pushed away the clouds of agitation that had briefly darkened his handsome features. Once again his sunny disposition brightened the room.

"For a while today I was afraid I was going to have to settle for bread and water," she joked. "Of course, I'm still interested in going out with you." As she walked toward her bedroom, she called back over her shoulder, "What do you have planned?"

"A quick dinner and a movie?" His answer took the form of a question as he sought her approval.

"Sounds good. Which movie?" She closed the bedroom door and was pulling off her blouse when she heard his warm chuckle.

"How about the drive-in? They're showing a double feature of *Bambi* and *Dick Tracy*."

"How did you know *Bambi* was one of my favorite movies?" she shouted above the gurgle of running water filling the bathtub.

"Mine, too. I'm a sucker for all those old Disney movies." He heard her turn off the faucet and step into the tub. The sounds of water splashing over her body drove all the more innocent thoughts from his mind. Visions of cute little bunnies and shy skunks were replaced by the much more exciting mental image of her slender form, shiny and sleek as she covered it with soap.

"Whew," he exhaled sharply. In the past hour his emotions had run the full gamut from anxiety about her safety to relief at her arrival to anger at the idea of animals being tortured to being tormented himself by a rising desire for a woman whose favorite movie was *Bambi*. Lord, how was he ever going to survive his time with her?

Or live without her?

SIX

"It's even better than I remembered it," Jenny sighed, wiping the tears away as the closing scene of Bambi standing alone on a hill faded to the credits.

Garrett's arm that had been curving around her shoulders tightened, pulling her closer. Leaning over, he nuzzled his nose against her neck and asked, "Have you ever been twitterpated?"

"Not lately," she answered, very aware of the delicious shiver that streaked through her from the sensation of his warm breath caressing her skin. All through *Bambi* Garrett had been a perfect gentleman . . . too perfect. He had held her hand during the comical birth scene when Bambi met his forest friends for the first time. He had given her a napkin to use as a hanky when Bambi's mother died and he had put his comforting arm around her during the frantic forest fire.

"Would you like to be?" he persisted in a teasing tone, referring to the movie animals' term for falling in love.

Jenny wasn't sure how she should answer his question. If he was merely joking, it would sound silly if she should treat it seriously. On the other hand, if he was subtly testing her interest in him, what would happen if she was to admit that she was very attracted to him. Actually, as his teeth nibbled the skin along her collar bone, she was having trouble thinking clearly, much less trying to second guess his motives.

Garrett lifted his head and met her befuddled gaze with an uncharacteristic seriousness. "Maybe it's the weather. Maybe it's the season. Or maybe it's just because you're you. But whatever it is, I know how Bambi felt when he saw Faline's reflection in the stream. He wasn't looking for love and neither am I. But I want you, Jenny," he breathed huskily. "I know now where you got your nickname. You're driving me wild."

If Jenny had had trouble thinking of something to say before, she was totally speechless now. What did he want from her? A summer fling? A one-night stand? Other than their love for animals, she could see no mutual ground. And, more importantly, she heard no promises for a future.

But then what did she want from him? Was she ready to fall in love and commit herself to another relationship? Was she ready to compromise her life-style should he ask? Was the desire she felt for him with increasing intensity likely to develop into love or would it build to hurricane force, then fade away?

She had no answers. Each possibility generated more questions. And with the uncertainty came the fear . . . fear of making another painful mistake and being trapped into a lifestyle she hated.

Jenny lifted her hand and let her fingers stroke the square line of his jaw. Her hazel eyes softened as she returned his gaze. It was too soon . . . too unex-pected. She often acted on impulse, but not on mat-ters of the heart. Long ago she had learned not to fall in love with anyone or anything because as soon as they became an important part of her life, they would leave. And this was true with both the human and the wild creatures she became involved with. It was easier to enjoy them while they were with her and not let them into her heart. It was her insurance that she wouldn't be hurt.

"Unfortunately, life is not a Disney movie," she finally said, her voice touched with a wistful wryness. "People have to be more realistic and not fall in love with a reflection in a pool."

"My, my, aren't we cynical!" he exclaimed, ob-viously surprised at her answer. "Who or what took the fantasy out of your life?"

Jenny felt the conversation getting entirely too per-sonal. Dropping her hand and scooting back across Bob's threadbare seat covers, she chose to ignore his question by changing the subject. "The next movie is about to start. Why don't we make a quick trip to the concession stand?''

Garrett obligingly took the cue, giving up on his queries almost too easily. ''Sounds good to me. A drive-in movie wouldn't be a drive-in movie without a tub of popcorn and a super-size dill pickle.''

Instead of being pleased that he wasn't pressing her for some sort of answer, Jenny was perversely disappointed. Did she want a man to sweep her off her feet and not take ''no'' for an answer? ''That's ridiculous,'' she snorted, unaware she had spoken out loud until he looked at her curiously and asked,

''What's ridiculous?''

''Er . . . uh . . . you can't eat a pickle without salt.''

''Salt! Now *that's* ridiculous.''

They continued their good-natured squabbling all the way to the concession stand and while they were waiting their turn in line. Loaded down with enough popcorn, pickles, nachos, and soft drinks to keep themselves busy for the next feature, they returned to the truck.

''So, how'd it go last night?'' Pete asked as he took his turn washing the breakfast dishes in the sailboat's compact sink.

''It didn't,'' Garrett admitted, yanking on his sock with a little more vigor than was necessary. ''Not that I was planning on jumping in bed with her or anything.'' He paused, the other sock dangling from his hand. ''Actually, I don't know what I was planning. But then when I'm with Jenny plans don't mean much. I never know what's going to happen next.''

''Is that a complaint?''

''I'm not sure. It's different. I think it would take a while to get used to it, but it's not all bad. It's sort of exciting in a crazy, off-balanced way. But I don't know if I could survive on a steady diet of it.''

''Does that mean you're not going to hang around with the Wild Woman any more?''

Garrett's shoulders lifted in a helpless shrug and he flashed his friend a sheepish grin. ''I'm going over there as soon as I get through at the site today. In spite of all the negatives, I really like her. Her peculiarities make her interesting, more interesting than any woman I've dated in years . . . maybe ever.''

Pete rolled his eyes and passed Garrett a glance that clearly said he thought Jenny wasn't the only one who was crazy.

For the next week Garrett still tried to rationalize the fact that he couldn't wait for each day to end so he could leap on his motorcycle and head for Ranch Mucho Amistoso. For a man who loved his work so much that he usually put in twelve and fourteen hours a day while involved in a project, his present actions were highly unusual. He would catch himself glaring at his watch a dozen times each day, eager for five o'clock so he could see Jenny.

Jenny. Her very name produced a warm, happy feeling in the pit of his stomach. Or was it closer to his heart? Garrett wasn't sure he was ready to accept that what he felt for her was anything more than a physical attraction. He knew how to deal with a sexual desire, but he didn't have a clue how to handle an emotional passion.

Garrett. His name was synonymous with confusion. As Jenny went about her chores, feeding the animals, working with the horses, transferring the bobcats to an outside cage, and doctoring her sick patients, she found herself counting down the hours until she would hear the roar of his motorcycle speeding up the driveway. During the last few years Jenny had gotten into the habit of going to bed soon after dark and rising with the chickens early in the morning. However, since Garrett happened into her life, she and he would be together late each night, either going out to a movie, bowling, roller skating, or grocery shopping, or they would stay at her house, make cookies or fudge and spend the evening watching television or playing card games.

Jenny couldn't remember the last time she had had so much fun . . . wherein lay the rub. She had settled into a comfortable, if boring life after she moved back to the ranch. But now that she was spending time with Garrett and so thoroughly enjoying herself, she would more vividly feel his absence when he was gone. With so many creatures to care for, she had never imagined she would suffer from any feelings of loneliness. Now that she had something to compare it with, she suspected there would be a notable emptiness in both her days and her nights.

But she had accepted the inevitable. It was already June. In less than a month and a half, Garrett's sailboat would be motoring out of the harbor and heading southeast. More significantly, he would be heading out of her life . . . forever.

And Jenny still wasn't sure how much to invest in the relationship because of its temporary nature. The cozy evenings of sitting at the drive-in or on her couch with their kisses growing longer and more passionate, their hands getting bolder, their bodies demanding a resolution were beginning to leave her restless and hungry . . . hungry for Garrett's love.

Jenny steered Bob off the highway and up the crushed oyster shell-paved driveway leading to the barn. At the far corner of the field she could see a cloud of dust that meant Rusty had gotten the tractor to work at last. He had promised her that if she were to buy the seed, he would have the field ready for it by tomorrow. She had been doubtful, but while at the feed store, she had added a few bags of alfalfa hay seed to her purchases.

Glancing into the back of the truck at the pile of heavy sacks, she decided she would leave that for later and relieve Rusty in the field. After changing into a T-shirt and faded blue jean overalls whose legs had been cut off into shorts, Jenny put together a few sandwiches, a bag of chips, and a large jug of ice water and headed across the newly cleared field. Rusty had spent several days chopping down and hauling off the larger of the mesquite trees and prickly pear cactus.

Catching Rusty's attention, she motioned toward the food and pantomimed that she would take over the plowing while he took a rest. Rusty let the tractor roll to a stop, shifted it to neutral and disengaged the plow before jumping down and galloping toward her.

"See, I told you I could get her working," he boasted proudly. "Just look at those rows. Just look at that dirt. This stuff should grow anything."

"With a little water and a lot of luck," Jenny added. "I see you got the old windmill working again, too. You must have magic in those fingers."

"Nah," he denied, but she could see a hint of a blush beneath the layers of dirt on his cheeks. "I just like fixing things. I even cleaned out the water tank. With the steady winds we've been having, the windmill should have the tank full sometime today."

Jenny reached out and gave him an approving pat on his shoulder. "You done good, Rusty," she drawled affectionately. "The storm that blew you into my barn was lucky for me and my farm."

Rusty ducked his head and shuffled uncomfortably, obviously not accustomed to such praise. But Jenny could see he was moved by her words. She wondered about his past again. As close as they had gotten in the last few weeks, she still hadn't been able to unearth any personal information about him, but she refused to give up. He had become her pet project and she would not be satisfied until she helped him overcome his problems.

They spent the next two hours alternating turns on the tractor with each of them slowly tilling the rich dark soil for the length of two rows before getting a drink and taking a rest. The deafening noise of the tractor's diesel engine provided a sort of isolation booth. She had to pay a minimal amount of attention to keeping the tractor headed in a straight line, so that her mind was able to wander freely. And the subject on which it most often touched was Garrett.

Jenny couldn't seem to get him out of her thoughts, even when she should have been concentrating on something else. She looked down at her watch and had to wipe off a crust of dirt before she could see the time. He wasn't expected for another three hours. Three long hours. Three long, lonely hours.

With a shake of her head that sent her brown ponytail whisking against her cheeks, she chided herself to stop being so silly. Garrett was just a man. He had not been the first man in her life and he would not be the last. But even as she thought about him her heart did crazy little flipflops in her chest and tingles danced across her skin.

As she finished her turn, she adjusted all the levers and was in the process of climbing down when she felt a pair of hands wrap around each side of her waist. Startled, she turned her head so she could see over her shoulder and was both relieved and mortified to see it was Garrett. It made it even worse when he broke out laughing as soon as he saw her face.

"I've heard of mudpack facials, but this is ridiculous," he said, shouting to be heard. With his index finger he traced the curve of her cheek, then held his finger up so she could see just how thickly she was covered with the coarse, dark dirt.

"This is my secret beauty treatment," she yelled back. "But I think there must be an easier way to do it."

Gingerly he dropped a kiss on her dusty lips. "Honey, you don't need to go to all that trouble for little ol' me," he teased.

Jenny smiled and tossed her head. "I wouldn't go to so much trouble for anyone else. By the way, why are you here so early?"

"It sounds like you're not glad to see me." He dabbed at imaginary tears in pretended distress.

"Sure I'm glad to see you. But I'm not glad for you to see me like this. How do you always manage to see me at my worst? I really did plan on taking a bath before our date tonight."

He surveyed the portion of field that had been plowed and the part that remained to be done. "And I suppose a bath is out of the question until this job is finished, right?"

"Right."

"Well, move out of the way and let me take my turn. My motto has always been 'if you can't beat 'em, join 'em.' You two are making me feel much too clean."

"Do you know how to operate a tractor?" she shouted.

"You're asking a farm boy from Kansas if he

knows how to operate a tractor? I was running a combine before I could ride a bike.''

''It's all yours,'' she said, stepping aside and making a sweeping motion toward the idling tractor with her hands. ''I'll just find me a spot of shade and watch you work.''

Garrett roared off in a cloud of dust and a hearty ''Hi-ho Silver,'' causing Jenny to burst out laughing. Since there were no trees out in the middle of the field to provide relief from the sun's fierce heat, Jenny joined Rusty and Rags where they were sitting in the meager, patchwork patterned shade offered by the windmill. Rusty handed her a glass of cold water which she gratefully accepted as she sank down beside the boy and the dog.

''I hope he doesn't run over something with that tractor,'' Rusty muttered, suddenly moody.

Jenny cast him a curious sidelong look. ''He said he had driven farm equipment since he was a kid.'' They were silent for a moment before she added, ''Why don't you like Garrett? I know the two of you didn't hit it off for some reason, but you both seemed to be getting along better the last few days.''

Rusty shrugged with intentional nonchalance. ''I don't dislike him. It's just that . . .''

His voice trailed off and Jenny waited for a few seconds before prompting, ''Just what?''

He whirled and confronted her with a fervor that surprised her. ''It's just that he's no good for you. Can't you see he's just playing with you? This is a vacation for him, someplace to go after work for a good time.''

Jenny stiffened and faced him, her chin lifted imposingly. ''Who are you to say whether or not he's any good for me? How do you know how happy he makes me and how much I enjoy having him around?''

''Yeah, but for how long? He's using you.''

''If he is, then it's because I'm letting him. It's been a long time since I've had a man treat me like a queen, and I'm enjoying it.''

''It won't last,'' Rusty warned, the concern swimming in his dark brown eyes, eyes that had always reminded Jenny of a frightened fawn or a whipped puppy. But now they were looking at her with pity and it made her extremely uncomfortable and unreasonably angry.

''Of course it won't last,'' she snapped. ''Nothing ever does. Love, happiness, passion, possession, they're never forever. Who knows what's going to happen tomorrow. I can't live my life waiting for the perfect moment because it'll be gone before I know it. It's a hard, bitter lesson to learn. I've accepted that things change, but life goes on. And you should accept it, too. That's probably why you ran away from home, and yes, I know you're an underage runaway,'' she continued, uncharacteristically harsh because Rusty had stumbled on a sensitive subject she had chosen to ignore. ''You expected perfection and couldn't understand why your parents weren't like those on the Bill Cosby show. Part of growing up is learning what's within your grasp and what's not. You haven't run away from home; you've run away from the truth.''

Rusty stared at her, his expression stricken and a hint of tears shining accusingly. ''You don't know,'' he cried. ''You have no idea what you're talking about. My mother—'' His voice broke and he lurched to his feet. ''You don't know,'' he repeated before whirling away and fleeing toward the garage with Rags bounding at his heels.

His flight jolted Jenny back to sensibility. Shame and horror at the sharpness of her words swept over her and she drew her legs to her chest and dropped her head until her forehead rested on her knaes. What had she done? Rusty had only been offering her the best advice his limited experience could provide. And she had cut him off at the knees, whacking away at his defenses until he was left naked and vulnerable. ''How could I have been so cruel, so thoughtless?'' she admonished herself. He was trying so hard to help her and instead of thanking him for his compassion, she had slaughtered him.

She wouldn't blame him if, at this moment, he was packing his bags and planning on hitting the road. After the weeks he had spent at the ranch, she was no nearer to finding out about his past, but from his reactions today she knew it must be incredibly painful. Possibly he had escaped from an abusive situation or alcoholic parents. Jenny could have offered him the hope and the happiness he needed to set out on the long road of recovery and she had blown it.

Leaping to her feet, she sprinted across the field,

following his path. She had to stop him. She had to reassure him that he was needed here and it was her fault she was so snappish with him. Slightly out of breath, she rounded the corner and saw the door to his room was ajar. Stopping in the threshold, her heart broke at the sight before her.

Wadded clothing had been hastily stuffed into his backpack with a trail of dropped socks, underwear, and T-shirts stretching from the antique chest of drawers, across the floor to the bed. His intentions were obvious, but instead of hostilely facing her, he was sitting on the bed, his head cradled in his hands and his shoulders shaking with sobs, presenting the total picture of despair.

The last shred of her earlier aggravation melted away and she knelt in front of him and pulled him into her arms as if her were two instead of seventeen or eighteen. For several seconds he continued his silent weeping, until at last he lifted his head from her shoulder and self-consciously brushed away the telltale tears with the backs of his hands.

"I'm sorry," Jenny said, the anguish heavy in her voice. "I have no business acting like a two-bit psychologist. My degree is in veterinary medicine, not family counseling and I should learn to keep my mouth shut."

Rusty remained silent, but she could tell he was listening.

"I truly want to help you. If where you came from is too awful for you to return to, then we can get you placed in a foster home until you finish high school. I know some people who will listen and honestly try and find a workable solution.''

"It's obvious you don't want me to stay here," he muttered. "You're trying to get rid of me just like he did. Well, I don't have to stick around this place any more." With a pitiful show of pride, he straightened, pulling himself away from Jenny and stood up. With shaking hands that revealed the depth of his distress, he began trying to stuff the rest of his clothes into the backpack.

Jenny reached out and stilled his hands with hers. "You don't have to go," she stated softly. "I know that sooner or later you'll be ready to leave, but until then, you're welcome to stay."

He hesitated, then as if his knees wouldn't quite support his weight, he abruptly sat back down on the bed.

"I have no place to go," he admitted tremulously. He lifted his gaze to meet Jenny's. "But that's not the reason I want to stay. I really like it here. I like the animals and working on the tractor . . . and I like you. You've been so good to me. I don't want to leave. I can work harder, I promise. I won't eat so much. And I won't give you any more advice about your love life. Heck, what do I know about that anyway? It's just that I don't want to see him hurt you."

Jenny's gentle smile softened her words. "It's not that I don't appreciate your advice, but I've been through a lot alone. And I learned to survive because I don't let myself get too involved." She sighed.

"I'll admit Garrett has become an important part of my life. I enjoy every minute I get to spend with him and look forward to hearing that silly motorcycle of his. But I know he won't be here forever and I can handle it. I like him, but that's as far as it goes."

Rusty looked doubtful, but adhering to his new policy of not voicing his opinion about her and Garrett's relationship, he returned to the subject that was most important to him. "So, do you really want me to stay? Or are you just being nice?"

"I *really* want you to stay."

"And you won't turn me into the authorities?"

She returned his steady gaze. "I won't turn you in, but I would like you to think about taking me into your confidence. I promise not to play Freud, but I might help you find some answers. Okay?"

"I'll think about it," he agreed cautiously.

"Now, let's get these clothes refolded and put back into the drawers." Jenny picked up a pair of jeans and had them half-folded, when she dropped them and rushed toward the door. "Oh my gosh. We left Garrett out in the field all by himself. I'll bet he's wondering what happened to us. You stay here and clean up, and I'll go see how he's doing."

Lord, her life was turning into a three-ring circus, Jenny thought as she jogged back toward the field. Slightly reassured when she saw the cloud of dust still slowly moving several rows closer to the windmill, she slowed to a walk. As she neared him and he caught sight of her, he waved and flashed her that adorable crooked grin she had come to associate solely with him. His teeth looked abnormally white surrounded by his now extremely dirty face, and her heart twisted in her chest.

She hadn't been totally truthful with Rusty. Yes, she wanted him to stay and yes, she wanted to help him. But her feelings for Garrett were not as neutral as she had implied. A simple friendship would not cause this tumult of emotions to pulse through her as she watched him turn the tractor off, leap down, and stride toward her. And the more she was with him, the worse it got.

Not that she would give up any of the time they had left together. She could be realistic about the temporariness of their relationship, but she could also greedily grab the moments and cherish them in order to get as much happiness as possible with him before he was just a memory.

As much as she hated to admit it, she knew Rusty was right. Garrett would leave her. But she would deal with that when the time came.

SEVEN

"Why do I feel like Huckleberry Finn?" Garrett's question was more of a statement. Although his tone was serious, the twinkle in his eyes betrayed him. "You get me to volunteer and then you and Rusty disappear," he continued. "I'm puttering around, filling my lungs with dust and I look over here and even Rags has deserted me."

"Poor baby," Jenny cooed in exaggerated baby talk, reaching out to wipe the dirt off the end of his nose. "If him wasn't so filthy I would kiss him and make him better."

"Me! Filthy!" he exclaimed. "Have you looked in a mirror lately? I couldn't possibly be as dirty as you."

"All I can say is that you and I won't be going out

tonight. Not even McDonald's would let us in in the condition we're in right now."

Garrett's gaze shifted ominously from Jenny to the stock tank behind her. "So you think we both need to take a bath?"

Jenny tensed as she guessed his intentions. "You wouldn't dare," she challenged, emphasizing her statement with a toss of her ponytail.

His answer was a rakish lift of one of his golden eyebrows.

Jenny laughed at his unspoken threat, but she took a step backward in preparation for an escape. In spite of being poised to run, his lightning quick reflexes almost caught her by surprise.

Leaping toward her, he reached out, but grabbed only air as she whirled away. He had the advantage, however, because he was facing forward while she was backward and had to turn before running, so she had gone only a few steps before he caught up with her. In a playful cross between a bear hug and a tackle, they tumbled to the freshly plowed ground.

"This is not helping," she gasped between giggles as they wrestled and rolled, both of them getting dirtier than ever.

"It's time someone taught you some manners, young lady," he teased. "First you put me to work, then you insult me. And here I took off early and was planning on taking you out for a fancy dinner and a romantic walk on the beach. But no, you'd rather play in the dirt."

As he spoke he lifted her into his arms and stood

up, his superior height and strength overpowering her. The fact that they were both laughing so hard they could barely struggle eased his task. Her only defense was to try to find a ticklish spot somewhere on his lean, muscular body to cause him to weaken his hold.

"If you dump me in that tank, I'll take you with me," she warned.

"Hah!"

The tank was not quite as tall as his waist, so it wasn't difficult to swing her body out over the water. But Jenny was determined not to be the only one getting wet and she clung to him like a monkey to a banana tree. As he leaned over, trying to toss her in, she pulled him off balance. For a split second, he scrambled to regain his equilibrium, but Jenny held on and they both toppled in with a splash.

They surfaced at the same time, sputtering and choking. But they recovered quickly and began an impromptu game of tag, half-swimming, half-running inside the tank, leaping and splashing like playful dolphins. When Garrett finally caught her, she twisted away, pushing him directly beneath the windmill's spout.

"EEYOW . . . !" Garrett yelled as the icy spring water poured over him. The powerful South Texas sunshine had warmed the water in the tank until it was like a huge bathtub and the sudden cold shower had been shocking. Leveling a warning gaze at Jenny, he growled, "You're in trouble now." Slowly he advanced toward her, cutting off her exits with his outstretched arms.

The look in his eyes froze her in her tracks . . . but not out of fear. She saw there a growing awareness of their situation. As he sloshed closer until he was only inches in front of her, she felt herself taking deep, unsteady breaths while she waited for his next move. His sun-bleached blond hair clung wetly to his head. Water dripped from the tip of his nose and trickled along the sharp angles of his jawline. His shirt was plastered to his body and his slacks were molded to the muscular bulges of his thigh. But somehow instead of looking totally ridiculous, he looked unbelievably sexy.

He took another step forward and Jenny felt his chest brush lightly against the tips of her breasts. Her body reacted immediately, and the muscles of her stomach tightened in anticipation. A fraction of an inch at a time he seemed to float closer, the slight movement of the water acting as a caress against her suddenly heated skin. As his thighs pressed against hers she knew he was as affected by the sensuality of the moment as she, which only added to the tender ache that had been building deep inside her since the first time they had stood together in a body of water.

For a few long, electric seconds, he gazed down at her, taking in how fresh and beautiful she looked, almost like a water nymph rising from the sea. The fact that they were not standing in the sea, but in a cattle tank and she was not a fantasy but a warm, flesh and blood woman did not phase him. He lifted his hands to her face, threaded his fingers through the wet strands of her hair and pushed it back until he cradled her head in his palms. A thin layer of moisture still clung to her flushed skin and made her lips look shiny and incredibly inviting. Unable and unwilling to hold back any longer, he lowered his head toward hers until he felt the softness of her mouth beneath his.

Their kiss was long and feverish, so steamy that when Garrett lifted his head he was surprised to see the water hadn't been heated to the boiling point. He certainly had. His hands dropped to her shoulders and slid down her forearms until his thumbs rested against the fullness of her breasts. The water had made her T-shirt almost transparent and the denim bib of the cutoff overalls covered the strategic areas in a peekaboo type of way that only increased his excitement.

"Jenny . . . Jenny . . ." he murmured, searching her eyes for the depth of her response. "Do you have any idea what you do to me? You're wild and crazy and absolutely wonderful. I never know what to expect when I'm with you and it always turns into an unforgettable experience. When I was a kid we spent many a hot summer afternoon swimming in the cattle tanks back home, but it never felt like this."

Jenny's arms were still around his waist and he could feel the gentleness of her caress on his back. Instead of replying, she stood on her tiptoes and captured his lips in another lengthy, delicious kiss that left him even more shaken.

He hooked his index finger beneath the strap of her overalls and followed the edge of the material down her chest, then back up again, savoring the feel of her skin beneath the back of his hand. "Why is it you always seem to go swimming fully dressed? Right now, you are definitely wearing too many clothes."

"Then why don't we . . ." she began, but she didn't get to finish whatever it was she had meant to say as Rags, who had been running in circles around the tank, suddenly decided he had been ignored for too long and leaped over the three foot high sides, landing next to Garrett and Jenny with a noisy splash.

As soon as he hit the water he must have realized it was too deep for him to stand, but instead of swimming to the side and trying to get out, he swam toward Jenny and pushed his way between her and Garrett and climbed into their arms.

"It's a conspiracy," Garrett muttered. "Mother Nature simply does not want you and me to get together and she keeps sending her messengers to keep us apart." As if on cue, the goose who had been searching the freshly plowed soil for bugs and worms, decided to join them. With a vigorous flap of her huge wings that sent a stiff breeze in their direction, Mother settled comfortably on the disturbed surface of the water and proceeded to take a bath.

At the chagrined expression on Garrett's face, Jenny couldn't help but laugh. "She must have heard you say her name. I must say, you do seem to have a way with animals."

"Okay, that's it," he stated, lifting Rags over the edge of the tank, then leaning over until the dog could hop down on the other side. "You and I are going to get away from this madhouse. I can't seem to have you all to myself for more than a minute at a time."

"What did you have in mind?"

He gave her a slow, sexy wink. "How about a long, lazy day spent on my sailboat out in the Gulf? Unless you've adopted some seagulls, we should be relatively undisturbed and I will be able to show off my nautical skills . . . and maybe a few others . . . to you. All you need is a swimsuit, the smaller the better, and a toothbrush. What do you say?"

"You mean right now? Right this minute?"

"Yes, I do. Tomorrow's Saturday, so I don't have to go to work." He leaned over and gave her a meaningful kiss. "We'll take the boat out tonight and anchor it in a quiet cove. We'll have a quiet dinner, just the two of us, and sit on deck and count the stars . . . until we can think of something more exciting to count."

A tremble of anticipation swept through her, but even though it sounded like a wonderful, promising way to spend an evening, she had to think of her responsibilities. "I've got the evening chores to do, dinner to cook for Rusty, and tomorrow I was planning on taking a couple of the wild animals out to a friend's ranch and release them. Then on Sunday I have a horse show in San Antonio."

Garrett considered her answer for a second, then offered a solution. "I'm sure Rusty can handle the chores alone, I'll call for a pizza to be delivered for his dinner, and if you can put off going to the ranch until one day next week, we'll be back in plenty of time tomorrow evening for you to get ready for the horse show.''

It didn't take her long to decide that his was an offer she didn't want to refuse. She was glad she had spent the morning working with Sugar so he would be ready for the show. And Rusty could handle the chores and would probably prefer a pizza to her leftovers. ''I'll talk to Rusty and if he agrees to take my part of the work tonight, then I'll go.''

Their sodden clothes weighing pounds extra, Jenny and Garrett climbed out of the tank and slogged across the field, the dirt mixing with the water and packing on the soles of their shoes. Rusty was just walking out of the garage when they neared the house and he stopped and stared at them as if he couldn't quite believe his eyes.

''Don't ask,'' Jenny said, with a chuckle at his bemused expression. She went on to explain the plans, at least most of them, and asked for his acceptance. She could tell he wasn't thrilled, but it was more because of his concern for her than because of the extra work. However, he agreed and even perked up when Garrett promised to order a large pizza with whatever he wanted on it and a six pack of soft drinks.

Jenny took a quick bath while Garrett called the pizza place. When she returned to the kitchen with her hair freshly shampooed and blown dry and dressed in a pair of shorts and a dry T-shirt, Garrett decided he didn't want to ride all the way back to Corpus in his soggy condition, so he took his turn in the bathroom while Jenny threw his clothes in the washing machine.

"Garrett," she called, tapping on the closed bathroom door. "Your clothes won't be ready for about an hour and I don't have anything for you to wear except a bathrobe. I'm leaving it on the doorknob for you. Okay?"

"Okay," was his muffled reply. "I left a twenty dollar bill by the telephone. Why don't you take it to Rusty while I'm in here?"

A few minutes later Jenny was back in the kitchen, stirring together a hot mash for one of her recuperating patients when Garrett stepped into the doorway.

"Huhum," he cleared his throat loudly.

Jenny turned around to look at him and burst into laughter at his provocative pose. The white terry cloth kimono robe that was almost knee length on her was almost indecently short on him. One of his long, hairy legs was stretched out in front of him, his bare toes pointed as he pirouetted. "You look adorable," she said.

"Yes, don't I?" he agreed in a shrill falsetto voice. "It's goes well with my tan, don't you think? And the plunging neckline shows off my chest."

In spite of his posturing, he looked breathtakingly handsome. The white material did set off his tan and made his eyes look even bluer. His neatly combed hair was more the shade of polished gold, the pale wheat colored highlights toned down by its wetness.

Even dressed in her robe, he was unquestionably masculine.

Jenny heard the washing machine stop and she went to the screened-in back porch. She transferred their wet clothes from the washer to the dryer, set the timer and rejoined Garrett. "It'll take about forty-five minutes for your clothes to dry," she informed him as she took the glass of iced tea he had poured for her.

"What should we do while we wait?" he asked, wiggling his eyebrows lecherously.

"We could watch television or play cards."

"Strip poker?"

Her appraising gaze swept his scantily clad body. "I don't think you have much to lose."

"Maybe I won't lose."

"Or maybe you'd lose on purpose."

He smiled and reached out for her hand, then pulled her toward him. Gently removing the near-empty glass from her, he set it on the counter and curled his finger under her chin, lifting her face toward his. "I can guarantee I would rather see you undressed than myself."

He was leaning back against the edge of the cabinets and one more tug of her hand propelled her against him. Through the single layer of material, he left nothing to her imagination. All other thoughts drained out of her mind as she leaned against him, enjoying the feel of his firm strength against her softness. He kissed her; his hungry, teasing little nibbles, making her long for more. His hands reached down to cup the round curves of her buttocks as he held her closer. Her arms slipped around his neck and she clung to him with a desire that she was no longer able to deny.

Their kisses lengthened, drawing from the passion that was burning within each of them and combining it into one fiery, sensual emotion that consumed them both.

No words were necessary as he bent down and lifted her into his arms, then carried her into the bedroom. The fan in the corner hummed softly, drowning out the rural sounds and the drawn blinds shut out the sights of the outside world. Garrett and Jenny were wrapped up entirely in each other and no one or nothing else existed at that moment.

Garrett placed her back on her feet next to the bed, then let his hands slip under the bottom of her T-shirt and slide over her smooth, warm skin until they reached her breasts. The thin lace of her bra provided no real barrier to his caress and she moaned as her nipples hardened at his touch.

"Jenny," he began, his voice husky and just a little shaky. "You're so special to me. But if you don't want this to go any further, you only have to say the word."

In answer her hands dropped to the belt of the robe, her fingers fumbling with the knot for a second before it loosened and she pushed the material aside. Appreciatively, she ran her palms up his ribcage, letting her extended fingers savor the layers of muscle that meshed together. A light sprinkling of soft blond hair tickled her hands as she ran them across his chest and on to his shoulders where she pushed the robe away until it slid down his arms and to the floor.

Jenny had always admired the beauty of nature, but the sight of Garrett's body was enough to take her breath away. Perfectly proportioned, he was lean and tanned except for a white strip around his hips to which her bold gaze was drawn. Had she been involved in his creation she wouldn't have changed a thing.

Garrett's hands, too, could not stay still. With a smooth, upward lift, he eased her shirt off over her head. In short order he had unsnapped her bra and disposed of it, then pulled her shorts and panties off her hips and let them fall down around her ankles. For a moment more their gazes lingered on each other, until he could resist no longer.

Sitting on the bed, he pulled her down beside him and they stretched out, side-by-side. His kisses started at her mouth, then trailed down her neck until his eager lips covered one of her nipples. As he drew it into his mouth, Jenny gasped and arched toward him. Her hands clenched, tightening on his arms, then moved around to stroke the smooth skin of his back. When his fingers moved down her stomach and added to the exquisite torture his body was performing on hers, it was more than she could bear. The tension twisted tighter within her, making her move against him, wanting him to continue, wanting him to satisfy the ache.

As if sensing she was ready, he moved over her and she sighed as she felt him move inside her. Gently at first, he let her get used to the feel of him. But he, too, had passed the point of holding back and he increased the tempo, waiting until he knew she had reached the ultimate pleasure point before letting himself go.

For long, dreamy moments they lay in each other's arms, waiting until their breathing steadied and their heartbeats slowed to a more measured pace before either of them spoke.

Jenny yawned and snuggled closer into the curve of his shoulder. In the distance the annoying buzz of the dryer alerted them that his clothes were ready, but neither of them moved.

"Do you want me to get your shirt out before it wrinkles?" she asked lazily.

"Wrinkles are in style now," he murmured his reply, his voice as relaxed as hers.

"What about the boat?"

"It's not going anywhere," he replied, nuzzling his cheek against the soft pillow of her hair. "It'll be there in the morning. Right now I don't want to move."

Jenny shifted slightly and yawned again. She couldn't remember the last time she had felt so completely satisfied and comfortable. She was glad they weren't going to leave soon because right now she was exactly where she wanted to be.

EIGHT

The vibrant rumble of thunder woke her. For a few hazy seconds, she thought the warm body next to hers was Rags. She didn't mind having the dog in the house and often let him spend the night inside, but he was definitely not allowed on the furniture. Rolling over to shoo the errant animal off the bed, she encountered the sobering, but very appealing sight of Garrett's tanned bare back.

The sheet had drifted down until it draped over the curve of his hipbone, leaving a large expanse of his smoothly tanned flesh visible to her inspection. The lightning that flashed whitely in the midnight sky silhouetted the strong line that began at his broad shoulders, flowed down to his trim waistline, then rose back to the angular curves of his hips.

The magnetism proved irresistible and she edged closer, snuggling against him. Her arm curled around his waist and, still asleep, his hand moved to capture hers and cradle it against his chest. Jenny drifted back into her dreams with a contented sigh.

When she awoke again it was raining in a pounding torrent. Jenny thought of the half-plowed field, but she knew that by morning the thirsty ground would have soaked in every drop of tonight's moisture. It had been almost a month since any rain had fallen on this part of South Texas which was normal during the summer. Unless a hurricane decided to pay a seasonal visit, "hot and dry" were the most common words used by weather forecasters at this time of year.

Jenny realized that at some point during her sleep, she and Garrett had shifted positions so that her back was now curled against the warm wall of his chest. The pleasant weight of one his arms rested across her body and his legs were entwined with hers. She knew this was something she could easily grow accustomed to. Unfortunately, there would not be enough time.

By the time she fell back asleep the rain had slowed to a steady, soothing drizzle. The sprinkle of drops on the roof and against the glass window panes was one of Jenny's favorite sounds. Not only did it bring a sense of peace, but it brought a temporary relief to the heat that lingered even after the sun had set.

It was still dark and still cool when she felt the

nuzzle of lips against her neck. The heat that quickly spread through her as his hands gently roused her body had nothing to do with the weather. Several minutes later she and Garrett lay panting, their passion once again spent.

"Why isn't that air conditioner turned on?" Garrett gasped, glancing toward the unit that sat silently in one of the bedroom windows.

"It broke a couple of summers ago and I haven't had a chance to get it fixed."

"You mean that measly little fan is all you have to get you through these murderous Texas summers?"

"Actually it's not too bad," she replied. "Keep in mind that this has been a particularly *heated* night and my fan is not usually called on to meet such a challenge."

With something between a groan and a growl, he rolled over and pinned her beneath him. As he looked into her eyes he commented, "I can't believe things get so warm with your other dates."

"Why would you say that?"

"Because I don't think you're the type of lady who gives her affections lightly."

He was absolutely correct, but Jenny wouldn't have dreamed of admitting it too easily. "That's an ironic statement coming from a man who probably has a woman in every port."

With the first tinges of pre-dawn light slipping into the room Jenny was able to see a serious expression darken Garrett's sky-blue eyes.

"No, Jenny. I don't have a woman in every port. You can believe me when I say that in spite of my footloose lifestyle, I am not a playboy and I don't get involved in relationships easily. I know I won't be around in any one spot for long and it wouldn't be fair to either the woman or myself."

Jenny was silent for a moment before she finally was able to ask, "So what happened to change your mind while you're in Corpus?"

He reached up and tenderly stroked some wayward strands of hair from her face. The handsomely masculine features of his face softened as his mouth stretched into an almost wistful smile. "*You* happened to me," he explained. "From the first moment I saw you, all sandy and wet, as you took care of Frankie, I was attracted to you. Because I was afraid of finding out just how well you and I would get along together, I stayed away as long as possible."

He lifted one shoulder in a little half shrug. "As you know, that wasn't long. And now I'm sorry I wasted those two weeks. I want to take advantage of all the time we can possibly have."

Jenny ached to ask him how long that would be, but she bit back the words. She had gone into this with her eyes wide open, knowing he would soon be gone. She couldn't start whining about that now.

"So where do we go from here, Jenny?" he asked as if reading her thoughts. "You know I have to leave in a little over a month. I'll stop by here when we finish the job in the Caribbean, but Pete just told me yesterday that our next job will be in San Francisco. It's not going to be an easy commute for either of us.''

She swallowed and managed to force out a deceptively steady smile. ''Your work is important to you and it's almost impossible for me to leave my animals for very long. You and I were lucky to have met. This will be a summer I'll never forget, but we don't need to be making any promises to each other. I'm not asking for anything like that.''

''I know you're not. But I don't want you to think this sort of thing happens all the time. I really do care for you . . . a lot.''

''And I think you're pretty terrific,'' she agreed. ''But we're both adults and once you leave, life will go on for both of us.''

A puzzled frown briefly creased his forehead, barely visible beneath the lock of straight blond hair that fell forward. ''As long as we both know what to expect,'' he finally added, ''then I guess neither of us will be hurt. If you were to tell me to leave right now and never come back, I would understand . . . but I wouldn't like it. You've made this trip to Texas something special.''

So it was all out in the open. He had given her a chance to end it now and if she were wise she would take it. A quick goodbye now shouldn't be too upsetting. But then, she would be giving up a whole month with him, which would also be painful. She truly enjoyed being with him and she couldn't see the harm in putting off their parting for a few more weeks. After all, she was used to goodbyes and no matter how attached she might have gotten to whatever it was she was releasing or selling, she had always been able to recover quickly. This shouldn't be all that different.

"Of course I'm not going to tell you to leave. You promised me a day on your boat and I'm going to hold you to that," she responded in what she hoped was a light tone. "Besides, I may need you to help us when we plant that field next week."

He hesitated a moment longer, as if there was something he still wanted to say. Apparently deciding to drop the subject, he looked at his watch, then dropped an affectionate kiss on her nose.

"Speaking of the boat, why don't we get an early start?" he suggested. "As soon as we get dressed, we can head toward the docks."

"Your clothes are probably wrinkled beyond hope."

"At least I won't have to wear your robe."

There was a golden twinkle in her eyes as she said mischievously, "I thought you looked pretty cute in that robe. It made me forget about supper last night."

"Which reminds me, I'm starving. If you're not too embarrassed to be seen with me in my wrinkled clothes, we can stop for breakfast on the way."

An hour and a half later Garrett steered Bob into the lot next to the wharf and parked.

"I don't see Pete's rental car anywhere," Garrett commented as he looked around at the other cars on

the lot. "Good, that means we'll be all alone today."
He passed her a suggestive look as he added, "I have
plans on finding a private cove where we can anchor
the boat and go swimming . . . without all those
clothes you seem to prefer."

"I brought my bikini."

"I had something else in mind."

"You mean skinny-dip?" she asked with feigned
shock.

"From one extreme to the other," he answered
with a roguish chuckle.

The sun was an orangish-gold ball just above the
horizon as they motored the sailboat out of the harbor
and into Corpus Christi Bay. After cutting through
Aransas Pass they moved into the Gulf of Mexico
and tacked to windward as they turned South. In a
zig-zag course that roughly followed the distant coast-
line of Padre Island, they sat on deck and watched
the seagulls feed on the schools of shrimp hungry
fish had chased to the surface of the water. Occasion-
ally the silently menacing triangle shaped dorsal fin
of a shark would slice through the small, choppy
waves, then disappear as suddenly as it had appeared.

Jenny leaned back against the cushions, watching
Garrett keep the boat under control with ease. She
didn't know much about sailing, but she did know it
wasn't easy to sail into the wind. With the skill of an
experienced sailor, as well as an inborn sixth sense,
he seemed to be able to guess the capricious moods
of the wind and adjust the sails accordingly so that
the boat never faltered or lost momentum.

"Somehow when you said you owned a sailboat I envisioned a little bitty thing . . . certainly not this great big yacht," she commented to him as they skimmed along at a rapid clip.

"I told you Pete and I plan on sailing around the world and although we could manage in a smaller boat, we decided to do it in style. When we first laid eyes on this beauty, we both fell in love with her."

"Your *dreamboat*, huh?"

He smiled and nodded. "And a sweeter, sleeker, more obedient lady I've never met before in my life." He passed an affectionate glance to Jenny and added, "Until I met you, of course."

"More obedient?" she echoed.

"No, I don't suppose that part fits you at all," he said. "You pretty much travel to the beat of your own drummer, don't you?"

"So do you."

He nodded and agreed, "Yes, I guess I do. It makes life more interesting, doesn't it?"

And more solitary, she thought, but aloud she said, "Why don't I fix us some coffee or cocoa or something. The wind's a little cool."

"Sounds good. You should find everything you need down in the galley."

Garrett shifted his gaze from the open sea to the delightful sight of Jenny's perfectly shaped derriere as she leaned over and walked down the half dozen steps into the cabin. When she was no longer in the line of his vision and he could hear the thud of cabinet doors and clatter of pans, he lifted his head and greedily sucked the salty air into his lungs. He loved his job, thoroughly enjoying the challenge of each new project. But it was only out on the open water that he felt totally relaxed and free. The feel of the spray stinging his skin, the breeze tousling his hair, and the screech of the seagulls that always followed, hoping to find a meal in the boat's wake brought him back to life. Nothing else could compare.

Well, almost nothing, he amended. The last few weeks had been wonderful, and last night . . . last night had been magic. He sensed that in Jenny he had met a kindred spirit. She was perhaps his perfect mate, the one woman who would understand his commitment to the protection and procreation of animal life. However, she was as locked to the land as he was to the sea. He hated the thought of leaving her behind. Yet, how could their lifestyles ever meld?

When the piercing scream echoed from the galley, followed quickly by the crash of a pot on the stove and an answering scream, then a third, Garrett leaped to his feet. Hesitating only long enough to secure the wheel and drop the anchor, he raced across the deck. His heart was pounding as all sorts of possibilities chased through his mind, each wrapped around his fear that Jenny had somehow been hurt.

Leaping down, not bothering with any of the steps, he landed on the vinyl covered floor inside the cabin, then slid to a surprised halt.

"What on earth are you doing here?" he asked.

"I live here, remember?" Pete answered.

Garrett's gaze moved from Pete to the pretty blonde woman standing behind his friend. He suddenly realized that neither Pete nor the blonde were dressed. Pete was holding the ends of a towel that was wrapped around his hips and the woman had hastily twisted a sheet around herself. Still not entirely understanding how the situation had occurred, Garrett looked at Jenny, whose wide eyes and flushed cheeks told him she was embarrassed beyond words.

"Where did the two of you come from?" Garrett hoped a few answers would clear up this confusion.

"My bedroom," Pete answered, unintentionally facetious.

"I meant, how did you get on the boat? I didn't see your car at the dock, so I figured you must have spent the night somewhere else."

"Susan and I went to a party last night and when we were leaving I noticed my car had a flat," Pete said. "I didn't want to fool with fixing it so late, so Susan said she would drop me off at the boat. And, as you can see, she decided to stay for awhile."

"But we've been at sea for over an hour. Didn't you two notice the movement?"

Pete glanced back at Susan and gave her a very personal smile. "We were up pretty late last night. I was having a terrific dream about sailing across the Atlantic when a noise from the galley woke me. I got up to investigate and came face-to-face with Jenny. Obviously we weren't expecting to see each other."

Everyone exchanged wary looks. Garrett reached

out and put his arm around Jenny's shoulders, offering her whatever support she might need, trying to ease her discomfort.

"So what time did we begin our excursion this morning?" Pete asked. "And where are we headed?"

"We've been underway since just about an hour after sunrise. And we had planned to make a day of it." For the first time since he had heard Jenny's scream, Garrett was struck by the humor of the situation and he could feel the corners of his mouth lifting into a grin. "So how does it feel to be hijacked? I hope the two of you didn't have any plans on the mainland today."

"Nothing that can't be changed," Pete replied. "I suppose we'll all have to do a little adjusting of our plans, won't we?"

Garrett gave Jenny's arm a meaningful squeeze. "Yes, I suppose we will."

"And the first thing I guess Susan and I should do is get dressed," Pete added.

As soon as they left the small room, Garrett turned to Jenny and apologized. "I know this isn't what we had in mind for today and I'm sorry about the confusion. I hope you don't mind too much. I'll make it up to you later."

"It was just such a shock to see Pete standing there when I hadn't expected anyone. And we apparently interrupted something . . . you know."

He curled his finger under her chin and lifted her face. "Yes, I know. And it's exactly what I was hoping would develop between you and me." His lips captured hers in a slow kiss that was filled with both passion and disappointment.

"I suppose this means I'll have to wear my bikini," she murmured as he slowly pulled his head away.

"You're darn right you will," he responded, his expression more chagrined than before as he considered what all he would be missing.

Garrett helped Jenny clean up the spilled water, then they returned to the deck where he lifted the anchor and adjusted the sails to catch the wind. By the time Pete and Susan joined them above board, Jenny and Garrett were able to laugh about the turn of events.

A few hours later Jenny realized she was having a wonderful time. She discovered Susan was bright and articulate, and Pete was even more witty and charming than she had remembered. The awkwardness of the situation quickly disappeared. Garrett and Pete took turns at the wheel while the others relaxed in the sunshine and sipped cold drinks. A light-hearted patter kept the conversation lively and interesting.

They anchored off shore of a small island that was exposed by a low tide. After packing their lunch in plastic bags and tying it onto a life preserver, the two couples dove over the side of the boat and swam to shore with Garrett pulling their lunch along with a tow line.

The sounds of their splashing and laughter disturbed a flock of flamingoes, who rose off the sandy mound with a frantic flapping of their wings and flew away in a pink cloud. The seagulls were not so reticent and persistently circled the picnickers. Some of the noisy white birds even grew bold enough to swoop down and take bread crusts from Jenny's outstretched fingers.

"I knew you'd have those birds eating out of your hand before the day was over," Garrett teased.

"And birds aren't the only things eating out of her hand," Pete said, sliding a knowing glance at his friend.

Garrett rolled onto his back and stretched out on the sand with his head resting in Jenny's lap. Obligingly she dropped green grapes, one at a time, into his open mouth. After chewing and swallowing a mouthful, and allowing a dramatic pause to lapse, Garrett replied, "I don't have any idea what you mean. You would never catch me doing something so domesticated."

Everyone laughed, but Jenny's was a little forced. Curious about Susan's plans with Pete, she asked in a joking tone, "What are we going to do for entertainment once these two wild and crazy guys set sail at the end of July?"

"I still have a year left before I get my master's degree, so I suppose I'll be heading back to Austin a few weeks after he leaves which won't give me much time to miss him," Susan answered, tossing a grape at Pete in a playful taunt.

"You're a senior at the University of Texas?" Garrett prompted in a grape muffled voice.

"*The* University," Susan confirmed proudly.

"I beg your pardon," Jenny spoke up in immediate defense at the subtle slur upon her own alma mater.

"Uh oh," Garrett groaned. "We've hit a topic that can't be discussed in the great state of Texas. Pete, it seems your lady and my lady are arch collegiate rivals. Jenny is a graduate of Texas A&M."

"Whoops. We'd better change the subject to something safe like religion or politics," Pete said. "In fact, I think Susan and I would love to take a walk right now, wouldn't we, Susan?" As he spoke he stood up and pulled a reluctant Susan to her feet.

"I believe we could have continued the conversation without coming to blows," Jenny said after Pete and Susan were several yards away.

"I have no doubt that you could, but I was afraid someone would start with the Aggie jokes and I would have to hold you back. Not that I ever mind holding you, but I would prefer that it were under more friendly circumstances . . . like now." With a twist of his body, he pulled her down so that she was laying on top of him.

The midday sun had quickly dried their swimsuits and heated their partially bare bodies. Wherever Jenny's skin touched his, it was like warm silk rubbing together with the powdery white sand as soft as talcum powder.

"Ummm, this is nice," Garrett murmured with a happy sigh as he wrapped his arms around her and held her close. "Too bad we have company or we could lay in the surf and make love like Burt Lancaster and Deborah Kerr."

"That scene was so sexy. I think making love in the water would be incredibly sensual," she responded as she rubbed her cheek against his and planted little kisses along the curve of his jaw.

Garrett groaned and this time it was more from frustration. "Jen, don't talk like that. I am already tempted to throw you over my shoulder, swim back to the boat and sail away, leaving Pete and Susan behind for a few hours. I wanted today to be perfect and here we are sharing it with another couple who would probably prefer to be alone, also."

"Just one of life's ironies."

"Yes, like the fact that you and I met at this point in our lives," Garrett commented thoughtfully. "It would be so simple if we were both still in college or if one of us weren't so deeply involved with our careers."

She didn't speak, but nodded her agreement, breathing in the sun-fresh fragrance of his skin and letting her fingers stroke the softness of his golden hair. He turned his face toward hers and let their lips meet in a lingering, bittersweet kiss. If he noticed that it tasted saltier than it should, he didn't mention it and Jenny hoped the brisk wind would dry the tears that had appeared out of nowhere before he opened his eyes.

It was after dark when the battered old pickup

truck turned into the driveway and parked next to the gate. It had been a lazy, unenergetic type of day, but Jenny was totally exhausted as she and Garrett walked toward the house.

"I really should pack Sugar and Taffy's gear tonight," she said without real conviction. "If I don't, then I'll have to get up an hour earlier in the morning."

"If you don't run me off tonight, I'll get up with you and help," he offered after dropping a kiss on her forehead. "I may not know much about horses, but I can handle grunt work."

She looked at him, her feelings of gratitude mixed with pleasure because he wasn't going to just drop her at her door and leave. She had been hoping she wouldn't have to say goodbye so soon, but the unpredictability of their relationship left her with no guarantees.

"Help is one offer I never turn down." She wanted to add that even more than that, she wouldn't have wanted to turn down his offer for another night with him, but she decided it was something she might later regret voicing. Instead she said, "As long as you don't mind being a little warm."

His hand dropped down to give her an affectionate pat on her fanny. "I have no complaints about the heat when I'm with you. Although I think I'll see if Rusty and I can check out that air conditioner while you're taking a bath."

As she relaxed in a tub filled with lukewarm water and bubbles, she could hear the muffled conversation and clatter of tools coming from the bedroom. She took her time, rousing from a half-sleep at the sound of the air conditioner's motor grinding into action and a cheer from Rusty and Garrett.

She didn't know whether to give credit to the unaccustomed coolness or Garrett's comforting presence, but she slept like a baby all night long, waking only when her alarm insisted. Garrett shifted, cuddling her closer, and somehow, in spite of all the chores she knew she must do to prepare for the show, he managed to convince her she should stay in bed a few minutes longer.

They worked well together, easily managing to load all the equipment, feed, and both horses into the trailer that had been hitched to Bob. While Garrett cooked a couple of bacon and egg sandwiches to eat on the road, Jenny packed her costumes into garment bags and hung them in the small tack room at the front of the trailer.

It was a two to two and a half hour drive to San Antonio in a normal vehicle and a three hour drive in Bob, so that it was almost nine A.M. when they arrived at the show grounds. The miniature horse classes weren't scheduled to begin until noon so she had plenty of time to register and get everyone settled in their stalls.

"I've got to change into my costume now, so would you mind combing Taffy's mane?"

Garrett took the comb and looked down at the tiny palomino. It was quite a contrast between the six foot tall man and the thirty inch tall horse. He felt just a

little bit silly as he knelt down on the ground and
smoothed the tangles out of Taffy's platinum-colored
mane. As if sensing his discomfort the horse twisted
her head around and nuzzled Garrett's neck with her
teacup-size nose. With a whoosh, she blew a breath
of warm air against his skin.

"I can't leave you alone for a minute before I
come back and find you flirting with another female."

He chuckled and pivoted around to face Jenny. But
before he could speak, his eyes widened in surprise.
"What on earth are you wearing?"

She looked down at the low cut, fitted red velvet
bodice and the yards of diaphanous scarlet hued silky-
looking material swirling around her body. "You
don't like my costume?" she asked, a twinkle turning her hazel eyes a warm golden color.

"You look like a cross between 'I Dream of Jean-
nie' and a belly dancer."

Jenny adjusted the loose belt of sparkling coins
that hung around her hips and fluffed out the legs of
her pantaloons. The light summer breeze played with
the long scarves that were attached to a small crown
on her head. Tiny golden slippers with curling toes
and a large rectangular, fringed shawl made out of
the same frothy scarflike cloth completed the outfit.

"If you think this looks odd, wait until you see
Taffy's." Jenny reached into the garment bag she
was carrying and pulled out a tiny equine version of
her outfit.

"I can't believe you're actually going to do that to
your horse. I thought you liked her."

"Don't be such a party pooper. She loves to dress up and have an audience cheer for her. Just watch how she perks up when she hears her bells." Jenny shook the red velvet halter that was decorated with tiny golden jingle bells. As she had promised, Taffy lifted her head and gave an excited whinny. Her silver dollar sized black polished hooves danced as Jenny fitted a scalloped chest piece and a miniature cloth-covered saddle on the horse's sleek bright gold colored body. After buckling the halter in place, Jenny fastened a drape of the scarflike material so that it cascaded in gossamer tiers around Taffy, mingling with the horse's silken tail to form a sort of train.

Taffy shook her head, sending the bells into a fairylike tinkling she so obviously enjoyed that Garrett had to admit he had been wrong.

"Okay, I suppose the two of you know more about this than I do. This is nothing like any horse show I've ever been to. But then Taffy is not like any horse I've ever known either. And I won't even mention how very unique her owner is."

The announcer called for the costume class over the loud speaker and Jenny snapped the lead rope to Taffy's halter. She handed Garrett a paper square with her entry number on it. "Would you clip this to the back of my costume, please?"

"I'm not sure there is enough material here," he muttered facetiously, but was able to secure it on the narrow strip of material that crossed Jenny's back.

"While I'm in the ring, would you keep an eye on Sugar? You can lead him closer if you want to watch."

"You bet I want to watch. I can't wait to see what everyone else is wearing."

It was almost as if Jenny could feel his gaze on her as she put Taffy through her paces. In the ring were entries dressed as nursery rhyme characters, football players, clowns, and an assortment of other creative costumes. It was a tough competition and Jenny felt lucky when she and Taffy were selected to line up for a final inspection. The judge inspected the animals, looking beneath the elaborate costumes to examine the horse's confirmation and watched carefully for any sign of bad temperament.

The judge handed his decision to the announcer. Jenny glanced toward the arena gate and saw Garrett standing there. As soon as he saw she was looking in his direction, he flashed her a wide grin and a positive "thumbs up" gesture. Jenny had always enjoyed these competitions. They were a lot of work and could be very expensive, but the publicity and championship points she was winning made it worth the effort. However, today, with Garrett helping her out, it was twice as much fun.

Jenny had never considered herself to be lonely. She was always so busy and had surrounded herself with so many affectionate warm bodies, even if they did belong to animals, that she hadn't truly missed the pleasure of human companionship. But Garrett had given her a crash course on just how much she had been missing for the last few years. He was the first man who had ever made her question whether or not she would be happy with her choices for the rest of her life.

". . . and in first place is Amistoso's Sweet Taffy of the Mucho Amistoso stables, owned and shown by Jennifer Grant."

Jenny realized the crowd was clapping and she leaped forward, leading Taffy to the judge's stand where she was handed a blue ribbon and a silver loving cup that was almost as large as her horse. Triumphantly they trotted toward the exit.

"You two were great!" Garrett exclaimed, wrapping Jenny in a bear hug that was more clumsy than affectionate because of the trophy between them and the two horses pressing against their legs.

They hurried back to the barn where Garrett undressed Taffy while Jenny changed from her harem costume to a more subdued outfit of black slacks, a tailored white blouse, and tall black boots.

"So what are you going to do with Sugar? He's not entered in a costume class is he?"

"No, he's in a confirmation class, so he won't be wearing anything but a halter. They look for horses with perfectly scaled down bodies, not just little ponies. They even measure them and they can't be taller than thirty-four inches at the withers. All of my horses are several inches shorter than that and have a strong strain of Arabian in them that gives them their small delicate features and graceful movement, and Sugar and Taffy are two of my best.''

"If I didn't know better, I would think Sugar was your favorite,'' Garrett said.

Jenny bent down and hugged the adorable white animal. "Sugar was one of my first babies and I've always been especially fond of him. Taffy is a couple of years younger and she hasn't quite developed the arena presence Sugar has, but she's coming along quite nicely. This is mostly a practice competition for her. There's a big show in Dallas in a couple of months and then the Houston Fat Stock Show in February, so I'm hoping she will get a little experience here to season her for those more important events. If my horses earn enough points, I can get a higher price for them and their babies.''

"You mean you would sell Sugar and Taffy?''

Jenny hesitated, then said, "Yes, of course I would, if the price was right. After all, I'm in the horse business. That's what I'm supposed to do . . . buy, train, and sell.''

"Why won't you ever admit you're attached to something?''

"I don't know what you're talking about.''

"Surely there's something or someone you care so much about that you don't want to let them go.''

"Sometimes I don't have any control over it. If the animals I take care of are wild, then they must be set free. If they're tame, then they must be commercial or they wouldn't be carrying their share of the load.''

Garrett shook his head. "But haven't you ever been tempted to keep one of them, regardless of the price?"

"Of course I have. But I have to be practical."

The announcer called for the next class and Jenny was glad for the excuse to escape. Growing too attached to something or someone was a subject she preferred not discussing with Garrett. He had no idea how close she had come to admitting that she was just a heartbeat away from telling him how much she would miss him and begging him not to leave. But since her admission would serve no purpose, she knew she would never speak of it to him. She would never want to hold him against his will.

Sugar was in fine form as he trotted along behind her as they circled the ring several times. As if aware of his superiority, he proudly stood with his hind legs stretched back in a show stance while the judges circled and studied him critically. Jenny tried to be objective, but she could see no flaw in the beautiful little stallion. How well she remembered the night he was born four years ago. Jenny had been watching his mother closely and had been sleeping in the barn when the coal black foal first came into the world. Even though she knew no foals except albinos were ever born white, she had been surprised when his dark coat gradually lightened until he was a flashy snow white. Not only was his color exceptional, but his body shape and size was an absolutely perfect miniaturization of a much larger Arabian. She had experimented with bloodlines and achieved some admirable results and even had another new foal by the same mare and stallion. But Sugar was, by far, her finest production.

The class of twenty-six was large and there were several very nice looking stallions in it. But Jenny was not really surprised when Sugar was awarded the Grand Championship, which brought her good mood back in full force. Every time he won he validated her program and her dedication to the refinement of the breed. Proudly she posed Sugar for the photographers and the little children who wanted to stroke his soft coat while Garrett began loading the equipment.

He seemed genuinely interested in the horse show procedure, so all the way home she explained her training methods, the bloodlines of her stock, and her plans for her stable. They were so involved in their conversation that they didn't notice the black Corvette parked in her driveway until she and Garrett had climbed out of the truck and were walking around to the back of the trailer to unload the horses.

"Jenny, sweetheart. I should have known you'd be at a horseshow."

Garrett and Jenny stopped and looked toward the source of the voice. With the door of the Corvette open, the interior light made the car visible in the darkness. A man stepped forward, swept Jenny into his arms, and gave her a big kiss.

"Denny, I wasn't expecting to see you tonight."

"Obviously not."

"Have you been here long?"

"No, I just drove up a couple of seconds before you did."

Garrett cleared his throat to remind her of his presence.

"Oh, Denny, I want you to meet Garrett. Garrett, this is Denny."

Garrett held out his hand and smiled. "Is this another brother?"

Denny looked amused. "No. I'm Jenny's fiance."

NINE

"Her fiance?" Garrett's smile froze on his face. When he turned to Jenny his voice was equally cold. This would explain Jenny's avoidance of discussing any future plans, but it would also change the whole complexion of their relationship. Moving in on another man's claim was not Garrett's style, regardless of his interest in the lady. "Your fiance? I don't believe you've ever mentioned that you were engaged."

"That's because I'm not," Jenny retorted in annoyance.

"You never gave me the ring back," Denny chimed in, obviously enjoying his role in this melodrama.

"That's because it was eaten by a goat. I told you

you could have it back if you wanted to have the goat spend the weekend in your bathroom.''

''I didn't want it that badly.''

''A goat ate your engagement ring?'' Garrett interrupted. ''Although I can't understand why that should come as any surprise.''

''It's not like it was a diamond or anything. In fact, I think it was some sort of rock Denny had found on a field trip and had mounted into a ring.''

''It had been in my family for years,'' Denny replied wryly. ''I was only nine when I found the rock and I saved it all those years until I met the right woman to give it to. And then she feeds it to a goat.''

''I did not feed it to a goat. He ate it off the table in the lab.''

''The fact is, you and I are still engaged until you give me back the ring,'' Denny teased.

''Don't listen to him,'' Jenny said to Garrett. ''We were in the same classes in veterinary school and when all of our friends began getting engaged and married, we thought we'd give it a try.''

''Yes, we were Jenny and Denny. Isn't that cute?'' Denny chuckled.

''Adorable,'' Garrett muttered.

Jenny ignored both of their remarks and continued, ''Luckily, we came to our senses before we actually went through with it.''

''It wasn't my idea to break up.''

''It was by mutual agreement,'' Jenny reminded him. ''We both knew we weren't really in love.''

"Speak for yourself. I think we would have done fine together. After all, we both became veterinarians. Did she tell you we set up a practice together after college? It was doing great until she decided to move down here." He looked back at Jenny. "I could still use a good partner."

"And I could spend my days clipping doberman's ears and fitting cocker spaniels for contact lenses. No thanks, pampered pets are not my interest. I'd rather take in strays and treat wild animals in the great outdoors than spend my days cooped up inside."

"All of my patients aren't overweight housepets. Just the other day I was called to the Houston zoo to take care of a giraffe with a broken neck, until a specialist could arrive."

"How on earth did he break his neck?"

"No one knows for certain, but they think he was leaning over the fence to reach some leaves when his head got caught, he became panicky and somehow fell down."

"Did he survive?"

"Of course. I'm a great doctor. His neck is in a cast, the longest one I've ever seen by the way, but in a few weeks he should be as good as new."

Jenny looked at him through squinted eyes. "I don't know whether to believe you or not. You've always had such a vivid imagination."

"I swear on my Corvette and my condo in Cozumel that it's the truth."

"Go ahead, rub it in," Jenny laughed. "Well, my house is certainly not a condo in Cozumel and my truck couldn't pass a Corvette if they were both going downhill and the Corvette was in park, but I'm quite happy with my life. Speaking of necks, what are you doing down in this neck of the woods anyway?''

"I've got a doggy dental convention to attend in Corpus, and I thought I'd drop in for a visit. Do you still have that couch that makes into a bed?''

"Sure do. You can go on in if you want to, but I've got to unload the horses and settle them for the night.'' Jenny reached over and took Garrett's hand. "You're not going to be leaving any time soon, are you?''

Garrett had been leaning against Bob's dented fender, watching the interplay between Jenny and Denny, and remaining, for the most part, silent. It was obvious that the two were good friends and the patter that passed between them might have lacked romance, but it contained genuine affection. Apparently they had been quite close at one time or they would never have considered marriage. The thought of just how close was like a knife twisting in Garrett's stomach. While he couldn't possibly expect a twenty-eight year old woman to be totally without experience, to actually meet a man with whom she might have been intimate was a very painful experience. Although Garrett had no real claims on Jenny, he truly hated the thought of her belonging to anyone else.

As he listened, the thought had crossed his mind that he would not be missed if he were to slip away.

But even as he was feeling ignored, he was aware of a hint of jealousy lurking below his normally dispassionate, non-possessive attitude. His anger that she hadn't told him about her engagement had been replaced by an overwhelming wave of relief that Denny was no longer an important part of her life. Or was he?

Had their relationship ended as she had said? Or was she still a little bit in love with her college sweetheart? Had Denny come to win her back? Was a broken heart the reason she refused to fall in love with man or beast?

Garrett was struck again by the realization that there was a depth beneath Jenny's cheerful, affectionate surface that he was still unable to penetrate. She cared . . . but not too much . . . and never forever, by her own words.

No, he wouldn't leave just yet. He would stick around until he found out some answers. He wouldn't let an old boyfriend from her past chase him off. Jenny was worth fighting for, even on a temporary basis. Sooner or later her shell would crack and he would find out why she could give everything but love. Garrett's worry at this point was whether or not it would happen before he set sail. And what would his leaving do to her? Would she even care? So far, even though he knew she truly liked being with him, she had never so much as hinted that she wished he could stay . . . permanently.

Leveling a challenging look at Denny, Garrett replied, "Yes, I'm going to stick around for a while longer this evening. I have no other plans and you'll probably need my help unhitching the trailer and unloading the gear."

Jenny smiled up at him, totally unaware of all the turmoil and questions crowding his thoughts. Lifting her hand to his face she let her fingertips caress the slight hollow of his cheek. "Thanks. I appreciate that."

"I'll help, too," Denny spoke up, obviously aware he was losing ground in this unofficial competition.

For a few seconds longer, Jenny's gaze remained locked with Garrett's, warm hazel eyes looking into intense blue ones before she stepped back and included Denny. "Okay, guys, let's get cracking. I've got two very tired horses who would probably like to get out and kick up their heels in the pasture."

"I know I'd like to kick up my heels," Denny commented.

"Down boy, or you'll get to sleep in the barn with Sugar and Taffy," Jenny threatened jokingly.

With all three of them working it didn't take but a half hour to groom and feed the horses, unload and clean out the trailer, and close everything up for the night. Rusty had already completed the rest of the chores, and from the sounds coming from the garage, he was spending his evening listening to the radio in his room.

Jenny poured some potato chips into a bowl, stirred up a cream cheese and chives dip and placed the snack on the table. Garrett put ice in the glasses and poured them all some tea while Denny carried his suitcase into the living room.

"This couch looks like George Washington could have slept on it," Denny called. "Are you sure there isn't room for me in the bedroom?"

Garrett and Jenny exchanged looks and simultaneously answered, "No, there isn't room."

Denny returned to the kitchen and sat down at the table across from Garrett.

"So how long have you known *my* Jenny?" Denny asked Garrett.

Jenny was standing at the stove, popping corn in a cast iron skillet, and gave Denny a reproving look over her shoulder. He chose to ignore her.

"Jenny and I met about a month and a half ago at the beach."

"At the beach, huh. You're not one of those aging surfer boys, are you?"

"Denny . . ." Jenny snapped in a low, warning tone.

"I've done a little surfing, but that's not why I was in Corpus," Garrett explained with polite patience. "I'm a marine biologist and I'm here to help with the construction of Sea-Free, a new laboratory and exhibition aquarium facility."

"So you won't be living in the area permanently?"

"No, my job keeps me moving every three or four months."

"Gee, that's too bad," Denny replied, but it was apparent from the gleam in his eyes and the tone of his voice that he was anything but disappointed.

It was then that Denny's intentions became crystal clear to Garrett. Jenny's ex-fiance hadn't come simply to go to a convention. He also had hopes of winning Jenny back. And he wasn't going to cut Garrett any slack. Denny had several advantages, including a past relationship with Jenny and a relatively close location. All he had to do was sit back and wait until Garrett was out of the picture, then move in.

Garrett scooted his chair back and walked restlessly over to where Jenny was pouring the popped corn into a large crockware bowl.

"So what's on the agenda tonight?" Denny asked cheerfully. "I suppose you still don't have cable out here in the wilderness, so movies are out of the question. How about some cards. We could play strip poker."

The reference to strip poker brought a reminiscent smile to Garrett's lips as he thought back to Friday evening when he and Jenny had been standing in this very spot, teetering on the edge of passion.

But his happiness was temporary as Denny added suggestively, "I haven't played that since college. We used to have some great times, didn't we Jenny?"

"You played strip poker with Denny in college?" Garrett sputtered in a voice low enough for Jenny's ears only.

Jenny threw him an exasperated look and said, with a hint of sarcasm, "You went to college. You should know that college kids *never* do such wild things."

He was silent for a moment, then asked, "Did you win?"

Jenny flashed a wide grin. "Of course. I'm a great poker player. You know what they say, 'Lucky at cards . . .' "

" ' . . . unlucky at love,' " he finished for her. "Well, maybe your luck has changed."

"Does that mean that I'll be unlucky at cards? Then maybe we had better play something else."

Garrett sighed. As usual, she was adroitly avoiding the subject of love, keeping the conversation light.

He thought it was ironic that they ended up playing Hearts. It rapidly moved from a friendly game of cards to cut-throat strategy with Garrett and Denny dropping the Queen of Spades on each other as often as they tossed verbal barbs.

After about an hour of this, Jenny threw down her cards and stood up. "Okay, you guys. That's it. I've had it. You two are more concerned about drawing blood than playing cards. I'm tired and I've got to get up early in the morning, so I'm going to bed. You can stay here all night and argue or go to bed with me."

"With you?" Denny asked hopefully.

"You get the couch," she repeated, pointing her finger at Denny. She walked around behind Garrett, bent down and dropped a kiss on his cheek, letting her lips linger long enough to whisper in his ear, "And you get the bed with me if you want to stay."

Standing up, she added, "Good night, guys. Turn off the lights and lock the door when you're finished playing whatever game it is you've been playing all evening." And with a casual wave, she swept from the room.

The two men didn't speak for a few minutes, with the only noise being the muffled sound of Jenny's bath water running and the slapping patter of the cards being shuffled together. Finally Garrett made a big show of yawning and stretching.

"Well, I guess I'll be going to bed, too," he said.

"Leaving so soon?" Denny asked innocently.

Garrett studied his opponent through narrowed eyes. Did Denny truly not suspect the intimacy of Jenny and Garrett's relationship, or was he taunting him? Garrett didn't want any shadows to be cast on Jenny's reputation and if Denny was unaware of the situation, would it be right for Garrett to make so obvious a statement as to march into Jenny's bedroom and shut the door? On the other hand, Garrett didn't feel comfortable with the thought of playing the gentleman, protecting Jenny's reputation, and returning to Corpus tonight instead of staying. That would mean leaving Denny alone with Jenny, and although Garrett thought Denny was probably a nice enough guy, he didn't trust him not to take advantage of the circumstances and try to convince Jenny she was still engaged to him.

It occurred to Garrett that he should trust Jenny enough to put Denny into his place, but at the moment, Garrett felt very insecure about their whole relationship. It was Jenny's nature to take in strays and feel sorry for the underdog. With Denny showing up on her doorstep, she might be tempted to take him in, especially if he gave her some sort of sob story.

"No, I'm not leaving just yet," he finally replied. "I thought I might stick around a while longer and . . ." he paused and passed a meaningful look to Denny, ". . . keep an eye on things."

"Another hand of Hearts then?" At Garrett's nod, Denny let him cut the cards, then dealt them both the correct number. "Yes, Jenny can be too trusting at times," Denny added as he studied his cards. "She always believes the best of people, which makes her an easy target. I would hate to see her get hurt."

"So would I."

They played for a while longer before Denny remarked, "She doesn't need an absentee boyfriend, you know. This place is too much work for her and she needs someone to either share the load or take her away from it all."

Garrett lifted his gaze from the cards in his hand to Denny's serious brown eyes. "So which is it you have in mind?" Garrett asked, deciding it was time they stopped beating around the bush.

Denny nodded, as if agreeing. "I've come to take her back to civilization," he admitted. "I should never have let her break it off after college, but I thought we both needed some breathing room and if I let her try her wings for a while she would get tired and come back to me."

The irony of that sentiment was not lost on Garrett. He had heard Jenny use almost that exact phrase so often when referring to her wild animals.

"But she's happy here," he interjected.

"She has a very big heart, but a very small pocket book. How much longer do you think she can keep this place afloat? It costs a lot of money to keep these animals fed and healthy and the state doesn't pay but a small percentage. She's going to work herself to death here and I'm going to try to talk her into moving back to Houston with me and setting up some sort of companion practice with mine. She could specialize in horses if she wanted. I've got a few acres behind my house and she could bring her horses."

"It sounds like you've got it all figured out."

"I've had a few years to think about it."

"Have you considered the possibility that Jenny might be truly happy here? And that she might hate living in Houston? And that she might not want to marry you?"

Denny shrugged. "Sure I've considered all those things. But I'll be honest with you and admit that I'm still in love with her. I've tried to forget her and haven't succeeded, so I decided it was worth a shot. What can she say but 'no'? And since I'm not the type of guy to take 'no' for an answer, then I'll keep working on her until she sees the logic of my offer."

"Jenny has never struck me as being particularly logical."

"Well, it's time she *was* logical for a change. She can't sacrifice her whole life for this place. What if she should get hurt or sick? Who would do all the work? Who would pay the bills?"

Garrett couldn't argue with that. He had been wondering the same thing.

"Just look at this house," Denny continued. "It hasn't been painted in years. And that old truck of hers is overdue for the junkyard. It's going to fall completely apart any day now. And she doesn't have enough money to buy a new one." He leaned back in his chair and motioned toward the driveway. "Did you notice that Corvette out there? It's a classic. Nineteen sixty-three. It used to be hers. Her brother got her a good deal on it before she left for A&M. It was the hottest car on campus. But when her grandparents died and she inherited this place, she needed the cash. When I found out she was going to sell it, I bought it from her, paid top dollar, too. She used that money to set up her horse business."

Through squinted eyes, he studied Garrett. "The point is that I'm here for her. I'm offering her a solution to her problems. What are you offering her?"

Garrett didn't have an answer. What *was* he offering her? A summer love affair? A promise to stop for a visit whenever he happened to sail by? A postcard from all the different places he would be working during the next few years?

There was only one thing he could offer her, but it wouldn't really be of any use to her at all.

"I love her," he stated simply, surprised that he should feel the urge to admit it to anyone, much less Denny.

"Join the crowd," Denny muttered. "It's your deal."

* * *

Before she even opened her eyes, she realized she was alone. There was no warmth coming from the other side of the bed and there was no body weight pressing down on the mattress other than her own. She rolled over and stared at the undisturbed pillow. Where was Garrett? Why hadn't he come to her?

Jenny stood up and pulled a robe around the frilly, shorty nightgown she had selected last night, hoping Garrett would think she looked sexy. Goodness knows, he had never seen her in anything even remotely sexy except her bikini. And he hadn't even been there to see her in her nightie.

She ran a comb through her hair, brushed her teeth, and left her bedroom. As she passed through the living room she noticed that Denny had already remade the couch and even folded the blankets. A burst of laughter from the kitchen caught her attention and she pushed open the door.

"Well good morning, Sleeping Beauty. And how was your night?" Denny's greeting brought on another round of laughter.

Jenny stared at the two men who were still sitting at the kitchen table just as she had left them last night. Except they looked worse for the wear. Garrett's blond hair was disheveled as if he had repeatedly drug his hands through it and there was a hint of dark circles beneath his bloodshot blue eyes. Denny looked even more exhausted.

"So what have you two been up to?"

"Me and Denny? Why we've been playing cards

all night long,'' Garrett answered, flashing her a loose, lopsided grin.

"You and Denny?" Jenny looked from one to the other and shook her head in bewilderment. "Are you drunk?"

"Are you kidding? There's nothing stronger than cocoa in this house," Denny retorted.

"Then what's the reason for this sudden change of heart? When I left you guys last night, you were exchanging verbal blows. I didn't expect you both to survive until daybreak. But I wake up and discover that you two are now bosom friends. What went on while I was asleep?"

"Nothing much. Like Gare said, we played cards and did a little talking. Funny thing, after we stopped trying to kill each other, we discovered we have a lot in common.''

"Gare?"

"That's right,'' Garrett confirmed. He stood up and wrapped his arms around her and whispered, "Sorry I left you alone all night, but Denny and I had a lot to discuss. Did you miss me?"

"Just a little,'' she teased. "The air conditioner is working great and I could have used a nice warm body to snuggle up against.''

"Not just any body, I hope,'' he growled.

"I certainly never expected to find you in here with Denny, laughing like loons. I think you both need some sleep.''

"I won't argue with you there,'' he said, then

added loud enough for Denny to hear, "I don't have a clue how I'm going to make it through the day."

"If you think you've got it bad, I've got to try to stay awake while they show films on how to fit dogs with dentures," Denny chuckled. "Now I'm going to take a shower and try to get my eyes to focus. It was nice meeting you, Gare. Maybe we'll bump into each other again some time."

"Anything's possible," Garrett replied.

"Time will tell," was Denny's cryptic reply.

Jenny had a feeling the conversation was way over her head. Either the men were too tired to make sense or they were conversing in some sort of secret code.

"Well, I've got to run," Garrett told her. He paused long enough to give her a long, lingering kiss and a pat on the behind, then he grabbed his motorcycle helmet and sprinted out the door, leaving Jenny wondering if there would be any plans for the evening.

"Are you going to come back here tonight?" Jenny asked Denny a few minutes later when he re-entered the kitchen. He looked properly professional in a business suit and carrying a briefcase in one hand. But she noted he was carrying his suitcase in the other.

"No, I don't think so. I had planned on staying a few days, but I'm going to get a hotel room in Corpus."

"But you're welcome here."

He reached out and twisted a lock of her reddish brown hair around his finger. "Yes, I know, Jenny.

But I don't think the time is right. Maybe I'll come for a visit in a couple of months and we can talk.''

Jenny walked him to the car and gave him a friendly goodbye kiss. She had a feeling she had gone to bed too soon and given Garrett and Denny a choice topic of conversation: herself. God only knew what they said about her. She hoped they had been kind. She had only been involved with two men in her entire life and fate had brought them together. It was an uncomfortable feeling, wondering what might have been discussed. Would Garrett understand that Denny had been a first love fling? Would Garrett care?

As Jenny changed into her usual daily uniform of jeans and a T-shirt, she mused on how her life would be different now if she had gone through with the marriage to Denny. No doubt they would not be worrying about finances. But would they have been happy? Jenny didn't think so. She and Denny had had fun and had remained good friends, but there had never been a burning passion between them. Perhaps he could have been satisfied with that, but she couldn't.

Her dream of an ideal man would be someone for whom she would be willing to give up everything— but another characteristic of an ideal man would be that he would never ask her to. The warmth of Garrett's laughter, the security of his arms, the ec- stasy of his lovemaking combined into a package that came dangerously close to her ideal. For the last few weeks she had put the rest of her life on hold, doing just the basics to keep the ranch working while she spent every spare moment with him. He had become an important part of her life and she knew she would miss him dreadfully when he left.

But would she be willing to give her ranch, her wild animals, and her little horses up for him? Even though he definitely hadn't asked her to give anything up, this was as close as she had ever come to being tempted.

Jenny pulled her hair back and secured it into a thick ponytail. She walked outside and was greeted by a happy Rags running circles around her legs and Mother waddling along behind, honking noisily. Out in the pasture the spring foals were dancing on their hind legs, playing and racing, and looking unbelievably cute. With their round dark eyes, tiny pointed ears, and slender, spindly legs, they looked like imaginary creatures, delicate fairies flittering around the meadow. .

In another pen, a fawn whose spots had almost faded was limping around on a leg that had been broken when she had been hit by a motorcycle. The shoulder to fetlock cast would soon be ready to be removed, and after her full mobility had returned, the fawn would be released back into the wild. The owl, his injuries fully healed, was now able to fly around the huge screened enclosure she used for an aviary, but because of the baby chickens and a new litter of kittens someone had dropped off, Jenny dared not let the owl go here, but must take him to a ranch several miles away.

The bobcats had almost doubled in size and were

now able to catch and kill their own meals. Another month and they, too, would be ready to be freed. And Jenny had no doubt that their cage would not remain empty long. There would soon be something else to take their place.

Her smile was both affectionate and wistful. These animals were her family. They depended on her. She cared for them and helped them get fat and healthy. And then they left. It was the same with Garrett. Even if he should decide to stay with her for a while longer, eventually he, like all the others, would leave.

They always did.

TEN

Jenny sat at the kitchen table drinking a glass of iced tea, trying to find some relief from the heat. She glanced at the drugstore calendar hanging on the wall. The month of June had passed with bittersweet quickness and already it was mid-July. The summer was half over and Jenny couldn't recall where the time had gone.

Garrett had become a permanent fixture. Even Rusty seemed to have accepted him as a friend rather than a foe. The three of them went on the bi-weekly shopping trips together, sharing the work and getting to know one another better. And they had spent an entire Saturday picnicking and horseback riding, on regular-size horses, at a huge ranch in South Texas where Jenny had taken the owl, the bobcats, and a jackrabbit she had helped recover from an amputated foot and released them. As they drove Bob over the game preserve, finding three distant spots to release the three sets of animals, Jenny, Garrett, and Rusty had laughed and joked with the ease of old friends . . . or a very close family. It was at such times that Jenny could easily imagine how nice it would be if that were the case.

She had still not given up on finding out about Rusty's past, but she was not pursuing it with such zeal as before. And she still waited for Garrett to press her for some sort of commitment, but he never had. He seemed perfectly pleased with things the way they were—pleasant, affectionate, comfortable . . . and temporary.

Jenny heard Rags' bark seconds before the sounds of a car in the driveway alerted her she had a visitor. She wasn't expecting anyone, but drop-ins weren't too uncommon. When she went outside, she noted the car that was parked in the driveway was anything but common. A silver-blue Rolls Royce sparkled in the sunshine, looking distinctively out of place next to the rusty, battered body of Bob. Even more bizarre was the fact that behind the luxuy car was hitched a scaled-down horse trailer with the words "Mon Petite Parfait" painted in gold script on its side.

Halfway expecting a chauffeur to leap out and open the doors, she was a little surprised when a tall, attractive man stepped out of the driver's seat and walked toward her, his hand extended.

"My name is Jacques Larson and I'm looking for Miss Jennifer Grant."

"I'm Jennifer Grant. How may I help you?"

"Ah, Miss Grant. I have driven halfway across the country to find you. Your reputation as a woman who selects and produces horses of exceptional quality has preceeded you."

Jenny wasn't sure how to interpret his statement, whether he meant she was of exceptional quality or her horses. Either way, she recognized his name as well as the name of his stables, both of which were spoken of highly on the show circuit.

"You're from California, aren't you?" she asked, pulling her hand away from his possessive hold. Even without his charming accent she would have guessed he was French by his flirtatious manner.

"Yes, our stables are located just south of Sacramento. We're a relatively young organization and have not been this far south to participate in any of your horseshows. But I can assure you, the Mucho Amistoso miniature horses are much talked about on the West Coast. And that is why I am here today."

"Would you like to come inside for something cold to drink?" Jenny asked, very flattered by the man's words of praise. She had worked hard to achieve recognition of her horses and to receive such compliments from her peers for her efforts was extremely rewarding.

"Actually, I would rather see your horses. Could we perhaps take a walk through the barn? I have heard you have a particularly exquisite white stallion."

Jenny's heart tightened in her chest. He could only be talking about Sugar. Well, she had received offers on him before and they had never been enough to justify the loss in stud service she would have by selling him, so she told herself not to worry.

As they walked down the dirt pathway, stopping at each stall to examine and discuss the horse inside it, Jenny's thoughts were mixed. Everything was as neat and professional as she could make it, but she was aware the overall condition of the ancient barn was probably shabby compared to what Jacques was accustomed to seeing. She could picture his barns as being the latest state-of-the-art facilities dedicated to the care and comfort of show horses, not a drafty old structure that had once housed a dairy.

She began to breathe easier as he hesitated for several moments next to one of her younger stallion's stalls. Chico was a flashy blood bay color with a long black mane and tail and black stockings. He made several favorable comments on the horse's excellent conformation and proportionate size, which led Jenny to believe that perhaps he would be more interested in Chico than Sugar.

But when they stopped at Sugar's stall, the man sighed and said "Magnifique" in such an awed voice that she knew she had a problem. Jacques bent down next to Sugar and ran his hands over the horse's flat back and rounded rump. His fingers circled Sugar's thin legs and he lifted each small black hoof. He peered into Sugar's large brown eyes and held the horse's mouth open and examined his teeth.

Sugar accepted this inspection with patience, however, he cast a questioning look at Jenny as if to ask her who this man was and what he wanted. Her only hope was that Jacques's offer would be too low for her to consider.

"He is everything they said and more. I really must have him," Jacques said when he stood up. With one last approving pat on Sugar's snow-white rump, he walked out of the stall and faced Jenny. "I usually can hide my feelings from an owner so I can get a better deal. But I can see that you have a personal feeling for your horses, so I won't do you the disservice of playing games. I will come directly to the point. I was planning on offering you fifteen thousand for him, sight unseen, but after meeting you and him, I will up my offer to twenty thousand. What do you say?"

What did she say? Jenny was overwhelmed. Twenty thousand dollars would feed her stock for several years. The mental picture of her check book came to mind. Just last week she had received an overdraft notice and had had to transfer the last five hundred dollars from her savings to her checking account. She had been counting on making between three to five thousand on this year's foals. It would have gotten her through the year, but there would have been nothing left.

"I see I have insulted you with my offer," Jacques said apologetically. "I am sorry. I should not have even mentioned it."

Jenny opened her mouth to assure him that he hadn't insulted her. Instead he had left her quite speechless. But he had given her an opening to reject his offer.

"Perhaps you will think better of me if I will increase the price to thirty thousand. A stallion as fine as your Sugar is worth every penny of that. Just as the name of my stables, Parfait, suggests, I appreciate perfection. And I will pay well for it."

Now Jenny truly was taken aback. There was no doubt she could use the money. In fact, it went deeper than that. She *needed* the money. Besides the food bills, there were bills for medicines, bills for the hay seed, and taxes on the property, not to mention food for herself and Rusty and their utility bills. And as loyal as she was to Bob, she had to admit that he was probably on his last wheels.

"No, I can see thirty thousand is not enough for your horse," Jacques continued when she still didn't answer. He reached into his pocket and pulled out a check book. "I have with me drafts from my bank totaling thirty-five thousand dollars. I will sign them over to you for your wonderful stallion and I will also add to the contract that you may either use or sell five stud services per year. Would that make it more palatable? I know you will miss him, but I can assure you he will receive only the finest care and training. I am not one of those absentee owners. I take an active part in my horses' lives and give you my promise he will never be unhappy or mistreated. I have the facilities and finances to make him a world-known grand champion, as he deserves. And I will give your stables credit which should, in turn, increase your own income." He paused, his lips spread into a friendly, yet confident smile.

Jenny, who was always practical and who had made it her policy to not get too attached to anything, was having difficulty letting go. Sugar lifted his small head and nudged her hand with his velvety soft muzzle as an affectionate nicker rumbled deep in his throat. "Could you give me a minute? I'll meet you outside with my decision."

"Certainly. If you don't mind, I will go to the pasture and look at your foals."

Jenny nodded, then waited until he was out of sight before she opened the stall door and knelt in the straw next to Sugar. She scratched his neck behind the curve of his jaw, just where he liked it the most and he leaned against her like an adoring child. "Oh, Sugar. What am I going to do? I have too many decisions in my life, too many others to think of, and too little time." With a sob, she threw her arms around him and buried her face in his thick, silky mane.

Garrett found her in Sugar's stall hours later. She was busily working, shoveling the old straw into a wheel barrow.

"Need any help?" he asked.

"No, I'm almost finished here. As soon as I spread clean straw, I'm going to move Chico down here."

"Where's Sugar?"

Jenny swallowed around the lump in her throat and answered. "He's gone. I sold him today."

The silence became so thick and heavy that she sneaked a peek at Garrett's expression over her shoulder. He was obviously stunned. "You sold Sugar? I thought he was your favorite."

"He was. But he's gone to a really fine stable where he'll get a lot more exposure to a higher class of shows than I could take him to."

"So big deal! He loved you and you loved him, so why sell him?"

She threw the shovel down and whirled around to face him. "Because I needed the money, dammit."

He seemed shocked, as much by her unexpected curse as by her exclamation. "I can't believe you did it," he muttered.

"I had no choice. I was offered a great deal of money and Sugar was, after all, just a horse."

"Just a horse?" Garrett repeated. Shaking his head he said, "Jenny, sometimes I don't think I know you at all."

"Look, I don't want to argue about this. He was my horse and this is my ranch. I have to do what I have to do to make ends meet. In another week you're going to be sailing off into the wild blue yonder and I'll still be here with my bills."

'You have alternatives."

"Such as?"

He hesitated and she attributed his lack of response to a lack of answers.

"That's right. I don't have any options. If I sold this place and moved to the city, I would be miserable. And I could never afford to buy another ranch, even a smaller one. Or, of course, I could always get an eight to five job, which I would hate."

"There is one other choice."

She waited expectantly. "Which is . . . ?" she prompted.

"You could come with me."

All the air whooshed out of her lungs. For the second time today she was at a loss for words. She never thought she would hear him say it, and now that he had, she didn't know what to say. For the second time today she was enticed by an offer she didn't want to refuse.

But could she be happy with the life of a gypsy, even if she had Garrett at her side?

Before she could answer, she heard the sound of a car stopping outside the barn, followed by Rags' barks and the slam of a car door.

"Jenny, are you in there?"

She recognized her brother's voice and mentally added another curse about his timing. "We're back here, Jeff."

"I'm glad I caught you," Jeff said as he approached them. "What are your plans for the evening?"

She looked at Garrett, her eyebrows lifted quizzically. In answer, Garrett shrugged and shook his head.

"Nothing special," he answered. "I thought we'd run into town for a burger or something. And I'd like to stop at a store and get Rusty a new pair of shoes. I noticed his are getting pretty ragged."

Jenny was touched by his thoughtfulness and smiled up at him. She was also hoping that later they could continue their talk. She wasn't sure how she felt about his offer, but it definitely deserved more discussion.

"Good. It's nothing you can't put off until tomorrow," Jeff continued. "Jenny, I want you to go with me. We got a hot tip about a dog fight tonight and if it's true, we're going to need your help with the dogs. Some of them are probably going to need medication. How about it?"

"I'll get my bag," she said. Then almost as an afterthought, she glanced back at Garrett and asked, "You don't mind, do you?"

"No, let's go. I don't know how a marine biologist can help, but I'll do what I can. Now if they were using Siamese fighting fish, I'd be invaluable to you."

Jenny laughed and looped her arm through his. "I'm sure you'll be very helpful. And I'll even spring for dinner tonight after we're through."

After putting a few emergency supplies into a black bag, Jenny and Garrett jumped into her truck and followed Jeff in his patrol car as they wound through the backroads between Rockport and Corpus Christi. It was well after dark when they arrived at a secluded area surrounded by cultivated fields and patches of thick brush. Several dozen cars and pickup trucks were parked on both sides of the country road. Behind an old farmhouse, a big barn, whose design and age were similar to Jenny's, was ablaze with lights.

Jeff turned off his headlights and let his car roll almost silently to a stop at the end of the long driveway. Garrett pulled up behind him and whispered, "You get out here with Jeff. I'll park the truck and meet you in front of the barn."

Jenny nodded, then got out, opening and shutting Bob's squeaky door as quietly as possible.

"Are there any more officers coming?" she asked Jeff as they crept up the driveway.

"Yes, there should be a half dozen or so arriving any minute. We're going to wait outside until they get here. At these things everyone drinks too much and tempers are running too hot. I certainly wouldn't want to face this crowd alone."

They crouched in the shadows, listening to the cheers and curses coming from inside. Jenny cringed every time she heard the pained yelp of a dog or the clash of teeth combined with their growls as they fought, often to the death. Silently she prayed for the backup officers to hurry so fewer dogs would be injured.

Two men's voices rose above the rest as they apparently became involved in a heated argument. Jenny and Jeff jumped as the loud crack of a gunshot cut through the noise and several people in the barn screamed.

"Well, I guess I can't wait any longer. Let's hope they get here soon," Jeff hissed as he drew his own gun and double checked to see that it was fully loaded.

"Jeff," she whispered, gripping his arm with tense fingers. "Be careful."

"You, too. Stay out of sight until the police clear everyone out of the barn."

She nodded and swallowed her fear as he left the safety of the darkness and walked toward the barn.

But just before he stepped into the wide beam of light that poured out the open doorway, seven uniform-clad officers came up the driveway and joined him. After a brief conference, four of the policemen separated from the others, with two walking on each side of the barn and heading toward the back to block any other exits.

Jenny breathed a small sigh of relief and tried to make herself invisible as Jeff shouted, "The party's over. You're all under arrest. The building is surrounded. Please surrender quietly."

There was a moment of panicked silence with only the snarls and growls of the dogs continuing. Then it all broke loose as everyone rushed to the exits at once, pushing and shoving, trying to get away before they were caught and sent to jail.

For the next fifteen minutes, it was total chaos. Jenny hid behind a pile of discarded boxes, watching the action between the cracks. She wondered what had happened to Garrett. She hadn't seen him since he had driven off in Bob. Right now she wished he was here with her, but she was also hoping he hadn't gotten caught in the mad crush of humanity. The people were being loaded into paddy wagons that had been backed into the driveway while police wreckers were hauling off the parked cars, impounding them. She knew that because dog fighting was illegal, everyone involved, whether they had been participating or gambling on the outcome, would have charges filed against them.

When it finally seemed to be under control, Jenny

slipped out from her hiding spot and ran into the barn, fearing the worst. A couple dozen dogs were frantically trying to chew their way out of their cages, barking and growling at the dogs next to them, confused and frightened by the noise. Next to the pit, a severly injured dog lay on his side, while the two pit bulls still inside the shallow hole kept fighting. They had been bred for their killer instinct and neither dared back off . . . or wanted to. They had come to do battle, regardless of what was happening to their human audience.

The only man who had not bolted for the door stood helplessly, a leash dangling from his fingers as he watched the animals.

"Is one of those dogs yours?" Jenny asked.

"Yes, ma'am, the brindle one. And I ain't leaving without him. That other mutt'll kill him sure," the man answered, his concern genuine.

Jenny wasn't certain whether it was because he cared for his dog or was afraid to lose his investment, but whatever his reason, she needed his help.

"Can you get control of your dog if I grab the other one?"

He looked at her doubtfully. "I can take care of my dog, but I ain't so sure you can handle the other'n."

"You worry about yours and I'll worry about the black one."

She picked up a snare pole and adjusted the wire loop on the end as the man did the same on the other side of the pit. Glancing over at him she called,

"Ready?" At his nod, she leaned over and began trying to slip the wire noose around the black dog's neck. After several tries, she finally succeeded and pulled the slack out of the wire so that the noose tightened, gradually choking the dog so that his attention turned from his opponent to the simple act of trying to breathe.

The man had also caught his dog and pulled him to the edge of the pit where he snapped the leash on the brindle dog's collar, released the wire noose, then picked up his dog and carried him away. A policeman was waiting and after insisting the man put his dog into a cage, he escorted the man and his dog outside.

The black dog had quieted down and was ready to be reasonable, so Jenny loosened the noose slightly and lead him out of the pit, keeping a safe distance between them. She knew when a dog had reached such a fever pitch, he couldn't be trusted until he was either sedated or removed out of sight of the other dogs. Carefully, she guided the dog into an empty cage, slipped the noose off and shut the door.

She had begun a cage by cage visual examination of the dogs when the humane officer arrived.

"Hi, Jenny. Glad you're here," the man said as he followed her around the room. "I haven't seen you around lately."

"Hello, Fred. It's good to see you too, but I'd rather we didn't have to get together under these conditions. Can you believe people can be so cruel to animals?"

"I've been in this business for seventeen years and it never ceases to amaze me," Fred said. "So how many are in good enough condition to go with me and how many are you going to take?"

"It looks like we got here early enough so that they've only had a couple of fights. I just pulled that black dog out of the pit and he's pretty torn up. And there's a spotted one over there who doesn't look like he's going to make it. But the rest of them seem to be in good shape, or at least as good as any of these dogs ever are."

She looked at their lean, muscular bodies, their short coarse hair, and their dull eyes. Too often the dogs' owners gave them as little care and attention as possible, tying them outside in the hot sun with only a tiny shelter. Even those dogs that were prized for their skill and tenacity were expendible.

And their fate was even less certain. Often when their owners were convicted of illegal dog fighting, the dogs remained in the care of the humane department. But because of their aggressive, unpredictable behavior, they were often unadoptable and had to be destroyed. Jenny knew her attempts to doctor the dogs would probably be pointless because they, too, were doomed unless they showed signs that they could be rehabilitated. But she could no more walk away from an animal in pain than she could a human. Like a prisoner on death row, the pit bulls, too, might earn a reprieve and she would do her best to help them get well.

Fred began loading the healthy dogs into the back

of his truck while Jenny returned to the badly injured one. As she knelt next to him, he looked up at her, his eyes filled with pain, and with a whimper and a weak thump of his tail he seemed to be crying out for her to help him. Immediately she dug through her bag, prepared a shot and injected it into the loose skin on his shoulder. After only a few seconds, the mild anesthesia began taking effect and he relaxed so she could examine his wounds.

When Jeff returned an hour later she was still there, stitching a jagged wound closed on one of his legs.

"How is he, Sis?"

She leaned back on her heels and flexed her aching shoulders. She had been kneeling and holding her arms in almost the same position for so long that her muscles were burning. But she was smiling. "I think he's going to make it. It's going to be touch and go, but he's done fine so far. He's a real nice dog, and young enough that he might be able to change. I don't think he's overly vicious or he wouldn't be in this condition."

"Are you ready for me to take you home?"

Glancing down at her watch, she frowned. "I wonder what happened to Garrett? Did he ever show up outside?"

"I didn't see him. Maybe he heard the shot, saw the panic, and decided to get away before he got run over."

"That doesn't sound like him. I don't think he's very confrontational, but he wouldn't run away. Did you see Bob parked out there anywhere?"

"No, there are no cars out there but mine."

"Well that's really odd. Maybe he tried to find us and couldn't. He might have thought we left and went back to the ranch to find us."

Jeff shook his head tiredly. "Let's get going then. After I drop you off, I've got to go back to the station and work on the bookings. A few got away, but I think we took in about fifty people. I just hope we can make it stick. I'm sick and tired of risking my hide to break up these pit bull fights, then have some slick lawyer get them off."

They loaded the two dogs into his patrol car and made the relatively short drive to her ranch almost in silence. Just before they got there he commented, "I still don't have any leads on that kid you're hiding. I'm beginning to believe his parents don't want him back."

"I've had that impression all along."

"Has he ever given you any clues to his background?"

"Not really. I just know he doesn't believe he has anything to go back to. And maybe he doesn't. Maybe there isn't anyone." She sighed and leaned her head back against the headrest. "I know that I'd be sorry to see him leave, especially if I didn't believe he had someplace nice to go and someone to love him."

"Speaking of someone to love and someone you're going to be sorry to see leave . . . what is the status between you and Garrett? And I promise this will be between the two of us. I won't tell Mother anything."

Jenny passed him a skeptical look. "I'll bet. You

love to tell Mother about my love life so she won't ask too many questions about yours." But she was glad for the opportunity to talk about Garrett and during the last part of the ride she told her brother about her mixed feelings, her sale of Sugar, and Garrett's offer.

"I hate to sound like an overly protective brother, but has Garrett mentioned the word marriage?"

"Well, no," she answered thoughtfully, but quickly added, "We haven't really talked about anything that serious yet; we were going to talk tonight."

"You're considering giving up everything that's important to you for the *chance* he'll talk marriage?"

"Garrett's important to me."

Jeff shrugged. "It's your life. But it seems to me you've sacrificed a lot to get to the point you're at right now. You love your animals and your life."

"Yes, but I love Garrett, too."

"I hope that'll be enough for you."

Jeff helped her unload the dogs and settle them into the barn for the night. They were so concerned about the animals that it wasn't until they were walking toward the house that they realized the truck wasn't there.

"Now I really am worried about him. Where on earth could he be?" Jenny asked.

"I'll ask around the station and give you a call. Why don't you take a hot bath and get something to eat while you wait," Jeff suggested.

"You sound more like Mother every day," she teased, but her attempt at humor was half-hearted.

She was exhausted. But she still had to treat the black pit bull and she wanted to check again on the spotted one.

It was almost midnight before she heard the gravel crunch under the tires and knew that Garrett had finally arrived. She had still not made it into the house, but had just finished taking care of both dogs. Wiping her hands on a towel, she walked out of the barn, anxious to feel his arms around her and have time, at last, for their long overdue talk.

Instead of him greeting her with a smile, his expression was stony. Other than the time he had been upset about the porpoise experimentation, this was the only time she had seen him truly angry. And she suspected this anger was much worse than the previous one.

"What happened? Where have you been?" she asked.

Even in the filtered light from the barn she could see the muscle in his jaw tensing and flexing.

"I've been in jail," he stated flatly, tossing her the keys and turning toward his motorcycle.

She trotted along behind him, trying to catch up to his long strides. "I was worried about you."

"Yeah, so worried, you came down to bail me out. If it hadn't been for your brother, I'd still be rotting in that stinking cell." He straddled his motorcycle and knocked back the kickstand. "It may not bother you to get arrested, but it bothers me. I didn't like my first, and hopefully my last, stay in jail at all."

"Wait," she cried, reaching out and touching his arm. "I didn't know you were in jail. I looked for you and couldn't find you."

"Well, you didn't look too hard. I didn't go far. I hadn't even parked the truck when a cop mistook me for one of those crazy dog fighters and arrested me. They hauled me off to the slammer and impounded your truck. They wouldn't listen to any of my explanations, but I thought it would only be a little while before you would miss me and come down to the jail to straighten things out. But heck, I should have known, you'd be so wrapped up in your own world that I'm the low man on your totem pole of importance."

"It wasn't like that . . ." she began, then stopped, because there was a painful ring of truth in his words. She *had* forgotten about him while she was working on the spotted dog in the barn. It hadn't been anything personal, but she sensed nothing she could say would convince him of that.

"It doesn't matter any more." For the first time since he had arrived he looked directly into her eyes. "I'm sorry, too. I thought you were special. I thought you really cared about your animals . . . about me. But I was wrong. I thought you were able to hold back from getting too involved with your animals because you had a strong, practical outlook on wild things. I thought you could let go so easily because you had such a good grasp on reality. I thought you didn't give your love away capriciously because you were cautious and intelligent.

"But now I know that even though you might be

all of those things, most of all you're able to keep yourself detached because you have no heart."

Jenny drew back her hand as if she had been burned. She gasped, not so much at the harshness of his words, but the bleakness of his tone. "But, Garrett, I . . ."

"It's over, Jenny. I finished my part of the job today and I was going to tell you we could spend a few days together. But now I don't think that would be a good idea. I don't like being taken advantage of. Not any more. It's over," he repeated and turned on the key, sending the motorcycle's engine roaring to life. "I'm leaving. Goodbye."

"But, Garrett, I love you," she called, finishing her statement, but she knew he hadn't heard her as he spun out in the gravel and drove into the darkness. It was too late. Her time had run out. He was gone.

ELEVEN

He was gone.

Jenny was so tired and hurt, she felt numb. Stumbling into the house, she barely made it into the bedroom before her knees buckled and she fell across the bed. Oddly enough, although her insides were being torn apart, her eyes remained dry. She had known all along that he would leave. It should have come as no surprise.

For a while there, she had thought they might be able to find some middle ground. But his offer this evening had consisted of her changing her lifestyle entirely. That wasn't what she classified to be a compromise.

But even then she had wanted him badly enough to consider it. She had done the unforgivable, the unthinkable, the most stupid thing possible . . . she had let herself fall in love with him. And he was, for all practical purposes, a wild thing.

The cold breeze from the air conditioner blew across her flushed skin, reminding her of the passionate nights they had spent in this bed together. She remembered the Saturday a couple of weeks ago when she had awakened to the sound of the old paint being scraped off her house. Garrett had engineered the project of giving her house a much needed facelift and had drafted both Pete and Rusty into participating. By the end of the weekend, her house had a fresh coat of lemon yellow paint with white trim.

He had given her so much. But he had done it knowing that in the end he would be leaving her. And now his conscience was salved.

She tried to blame him and shrink him in her memory. But the truth was, he had given much more than he had taken, and he had always been totally honest with her. Of course she couldn't expect him to give up his lifestyle, not when his trip around the world was something he had been planning and saving for all his life. Just as she was a land animal, he was a sea creature. She thought of Frankie, stranded on the beach, out of his element and slowly dying beneath the brutal sun. That's how Garrett would have felt had she tightened the noose around his neck and pressured him to stay.

The old adage "If you love something set it free; if it comes back it's yours; if it doesn't, then it never did belong to you" kept running through her mind.

By not admitting her love and putting him on some sort of guilt trip, she had set him free. Now all she could do was wait to see if he would come back. But the ache in her heart told her he wouldn't.

The next morning she felt listless and she knew she must look as bad as she felt. Her eyes were swollen with unshed tears and her complexion was pale. Rusty seemed to hover around her, sensing her pain, but unaware of how to ease it. Finally, he marched up to where she was standing, leaning on the corral fence and watching the horses play.

"Uh, I know I promised to butt out and maybe I should keep my mouth shut, but when I heard the truck drive up last night I came outside to see what was going on." He cleared his throat nervously before continuing. "Well, I couldn't help but overhear your and Garrett's conversation and uh, I just want you to know that you won't be alone. I'll stay here with you and help you run this place."

Jenny was touched by his offer. But she knew it was time to clear the air. Twisting around until she was facing him, she said, "I'll make a deal with you, Rusty. If you'll be honest with me and tell me the truth about your family and why you've run away, I promise I'll do everything in my power to convince them you should stay here while you finish school. What grade are you in?"

"I had almost finished my junior year in high school," he admitted.

"See, that wasn't so difficult. Come on and tell me the rest so I can help you," she urged.

He hesitated, reluctant to reveal his secret, but as if he suddenly decided to trust her, it all spilled out.

"My father died when I was too young to remember, and I never knew my grandparents. Me and Mom were all alone in the world and we had it tough, but we survived. I got a job as soon as I could and Mom worked as much overtime as she could. She didn't have any time for dating or anything like that, so when she met a man at work, she must have been an easy target. They got married after only a few weeks. But instead of her life getting easier, it got harder. She hadn't known Mick had a drinking problem until after the wedding. And he was a mean drunk. He used to come home in the middle of the night and start beating on me and Mom for no reason at all."

Rusty's voice broke and his eyes darkened as he remembered. "He never did like me. I don't know why. I didn't try to pick fights or anything, but I hated what he was doing to my mother. Except I didn't know who to tell or what to do. And I couldn't leave her. I tried to get her to leave him, and she tried once, but he threatened to kill her if she tried again.

"Anyway, things would be okay for a while, but then they would get worse. He lost his job and Mom was supporting us all. I had to drop out of football and get a better job. I didn't tell Mom, but I was saving a little bit every week so we could escape from Mick and his craziness. But before I had enough,

Mom had a stroke and . . ." His voce broke. The memory, even now, was almost too painful to bear.

"Your mother died," Jenny finished for him.

He nodded, not trusting himself to speak.

"And you didn't want to stay with your stepfather, so you ran away."

Again he nodded. "I had nowhere to go, no one to turn to. I was scared of him and of what he might do, so I decided to run away. I went to the bank to withdraw my savings and found he had already cleaned it out, for booze, no doubt. I went back to the house and confronted him about it. He got mad and threw me out. It wasn't that I loved him or anything, but he was the only father I had ever known. So I left, hoping to make it to Houston or Dallas because I figured I could get a job as an auto mechanic there. But I didn't have much luck hitchhiking and that storm blew in. I was pretty tired so when I saw your barn, I decided to get some sleep and start early the next day. You know the rest." He roughly wiped the back of his hand across his eyes, then turned the full impact of his pleading brown eyes on her. "He doesn't want me around and he doesn't care what I do. Please let me stay. Don't make me go back because I'll just run away again. I'm almost eighteen and I don't have to stay with him any more."

Jenny considered the problem for a minute, then said, "I don't think you have anything to worry about. I'm sure that my brother can show up at your stepfather's house and convince him it would be in his best interests to let you go quietly or risk having the state press charges against him for child abuse. Actually, I don't think he'll put up much of a fuss because he hasn't even reported you missing, so he must be afraid of what you would tell the police.''

"Then you don't mind if I stay?"

"I'd be sorry if you left," she admitted. "But you have to agree to go to school. And if you do well, I could get you into the local 4-H Club and you could probably earn a scholarship. Does that sound fair?''

He nodded eagerly. "That sounds great.''

"Oh, and one more thing. I've come into a little money and I'm going to be looking for a new pickup truck. How would you like to take care of Bob for me?''

"Me? Drive Bob? You bet I would. I could have him running like a Mercedes in no time at all.''

"Good, then I'll go call my brother.''

"Uh, there's something else I wanted to talk to you about.''

"What?''

Again he shuffled around, apparently uncomfortable with the subject matter. "You know I didn't care much for Garrett at first. I thought he was just out for a good time. But I was wrong about him. He's crazy about you.''

"No, I don't think so.''

"Yes, he is. I'm positive. He even told me he was going to ask you to marry him and see if you wouldn't think about travelling with him for a few months out of the year.''

"He told you that?'' she echoed in disbelief.

"He asked me if I thought I could take care of this place while you were gone. The horses like me and I wouldn't have any problem with them, but I couldn't doctor the other animals. But if you weren't gone too long at a time, I could manage alone."

"I don't know . . ." she said skeptically.

Rusty gave her an encouraging smile and drew from his growing self-confidence to say, "I had hoped you two would come up with something permanent. Even though y'all aren't all that much older than me, it was almost like having a real family when we did things together."

Jenny's agreement was wistful. "Yes, it was nice."

"Maybe if you talked about it some more . . ."

"It's too late. He said it was over."

"And you didn't argue?"

"Of course not. I let him go. If he really cared, he wouldn't have left so easily."

Rusty gave her a concerned look. "You didn't *let* him go. You pushed him away. Maybe he felt like you were the one that didn't care."

An angry denial filled her mouth, but she couldn't spit it out. What if Rusty was right? Perhaps his viewpoint was objective enough to see the whole picture. Had she been so careful to avoid trying to possess Garrett that she had rejected him?

She had had to struggle through the years as she watched one after another of her favorite animals go. Even though she had tried not to love them, she had. It might have appeared that she didn't care, but sometimes it broke her heart. It had never gotten any easier. Selling Sugar had been the most difficult thing she had ever experienced . . . until Garrett left.

But if what Rusty said was true and Garrett had been thinking about marriage, then perhaps the future wasn't as bleak as it appeared. Maybe she and Garrett could talk through their problems and reach some sort of compromise. After all, what did she have to lose? If she let him sail away without at least a proper goodbye, then she would never know if she had missed her best chance at happiness or if she had thrown it away. She loved him and if he loved her, surely that was enough justification for a slight revision of her policy. Throwing all practicality aside, she decided that for once she would listen to her heart and not her head.

She reached up and pulled the rubber band out of her hair, then shook the thick brown strands loose around her shoulders. "Okay, Rusty. I'm going to give it my best shot. When he disappears over the horizon, he's going to know what he's leaving behind. I'm going to change into something a little less horsey and more unforgettable, jump in ol' Bob and head for the harbor. Maybe I'll stop by and pick up something for lunch. Then we could sail out into the bay so we could have some time alone." She continued rattling off plans as she headed toward the house at a quick jog.

Fifteen minutes later, she was dressed in a halter top she hoped he would find irresistibly sexy, a pair of white shorts, and leather sandals. She waved cheerfully at Rusty as she jumped into the truck, pumped the gas pedal, started the engine, shifted into reverse, and popped the clutch in her hurry to back down the driveway.

"Whoa, boy. We've got to make it to the docks in one piece, and I'm trusting you to make it in record time," she said, patting the dusty cracked dashboard as if the truck could understand. The trip to Corpus seemed to take an inordinately long time. When she stopped at the fried chicken take-out restaurant, the counter girl was unbearably slow. When the order was finally assembled and the girl rang in the wrong amount, Jenny tossed her a twenty dollar bill and, in a gesture that showed just how distracted she was, she told the girl to keep the change and hurried out the door.

All the way to Corpus Jenny had been remembering the warmth that had touched Garrett's eyes whenever he looked at her and the tenderness of his touch. She thought about his gentleness, his charming sense of humor, and the happiness she felt whenever she was with him. It didn't matter if he was gone for three months at a time as long as she knew he would be coming back to her. And sometimes, when Rusty wasn't too involved in school, she might be able to get away for a week or two to be with him.

For the first time, she felt confident they could make it work. It didn't have to end. She had found a love that could last forever.

The parking lot at the dock was full and she had to park a couple of blocks away. Her arms loaded with the food, she walked toward the slip, her pace increasing with each step. She couldn't wait to see him, to apologize, to tell him how much she loved him, to . . .

She stopped so suddenly, she almost stumbled. The slip was empty. *The Eagle and The Hawk* was gone.

Jenny whirled around and practically ran down the pier to the boathouse.

"The sailboat in slip one-twelve," she panted, trying to catch her breath and not drop the armload of food. "Is it still here? I mean, has it gone out for the day or have the owners left for good?"

The elderly man flipped through his log book and ran his finger down the page until he found number one hundred twelve. "Yep, it's gone. But I don't think it'll be coming back. They stopped by last night, paid their bill in full, and said they would be leaving today."

"Do you know how long ago they left?"

"Nope, not exactly. I don't come in until ten and they was gone before then." He glanced at his watch. "It's almost noon now, so that would make it at least two hours ago."

"Are you sure they won't be coming back?" she asked desperately, already knowing the answer and not wanting to accept it. But the very fact that Garrett had sailed without making any attempt to contact her one last time told her more clearly than words that he didn't have anything else to say to her. It truly was over.

"I can't see why they would. They didn't leave

anything behind that I know of. Nothing important, that is.''

"No, I suppose not. Nothing important,'' she mumbled, feeling dangerously close to tears. ''Here, would you like some chicken for lunch? It looks like I'm not going to be needing this.''

"Sure, missy. I love chicken.''

She practically dropped the food into his arms and fled. The tears started falling by the time she reached her truck. Yanking the door open, she tumbled inside and tried to fit the key into the ignition. But her fumbling fingers were useless and the keys fell to the floorboard. Resting her head on the top of the steering wheel, she let it all go, all the disappointment and the frustrations, all the pain at being left behind by the man she loved.

When she finally collected her wits enough so she could start the engine and drive away, she didn't want to go straight home. Bob seemed to turn, of his own will, toward the strip of beach where she had found Frankie that day over two months ago. There were hundreds of people there today, but they were all so busy having a good time that no one seemed to notice Jenny as she walked down to the water's edge.

For long lonely moments she stood, staring out to sea, hoping to catch a final glimpse of *The Eagle and The Hawk*'s blue and white sails. Dozens of sails dotted the horizon, but she didn't see the ones she was hoping for. Several hundred yards off shore a pair of dolphins swam, their silvery bodies sparkling in the sunlight as they arched out of the water.

Jenny wondered if it could possibly be Frankie and Annette. That would be the height of irony if on the day Garrett left her she should see the dolphin that had caused them to meet originally.

Slowly she sank to the sand. Crossing her legs, she drew them up until she could rest her chin on her knees. Hugging her legs tightly, she sat, thinking about what might have been and wishing she had one more chance.

The sun was setting behind her, taking with it the last brilliance of the day. Jenny lifted her head and looked around, startled to see almost everyone else had gone home. She had no idea how long she had sat there. Her muscles protested as she pushed herself up, telling her that they hadn't moved for hours.

As she drove back home, at a more sedate pace which Bob preferred, she realized that although she had thought through all the possibilities and probabilities of her situation, she was no closer to a solution than she had been at noon. One minute she would make plans to drive to Sea-Free and ask for Garrett's forwarding address. Perhaps if she wrote about her feelings, he would get in touch with her. But then she would decide to let nature take its course, and if he wanted to come back to her, he would.

She was at an all-time low when she pulled into her driveway. When she saw there was another pickup truck already there, she groaned. She was in no mood to entertain anyone. For a moment she considered backing out and hiding until they left, but she knew she had to face life sooner or later, and she might as well start now.

Not particularly eager, she climbed out of Bob, curiously circled the shiny new two-toned blue Ford pickup and walked through the gate toward her house. Even in the semidarkness it looked almost beautiful in its fresh coat of paint, and once again, the ache tugged at her heart. Would she ever be able to look around her and see all the things Garrett had helped her with, without feeling the pain of his loss?

"Good Lord, Jenny. Where have you been all day?"

Jenny shook her head. She had been thinking so much about Garrett that she thought she had heard his voice.

"Your nose is sunburned. If you've been having a great time at the beach while I've been sitting here waiting for you, I'm going to turn you over my knee and spank you."

Jenny looked up. Outlined in the glare of the porch light, a man whose broad shoulders, slim hips and long legs looked exactly like Garrett's stood on the back porch. She had a good imagination, but even she couldn't have imagined something so real.

"What are you doing here?" she asked bluntly, totally rattled by his unexpected presence.

"Well, that's not exactly the greeting I was hoping for. I had something more like hugs and kisses in mind."

Jenny's purse slipped from her fingers and she

threw herself into his arms. Covering his face in kisses, she said, "Is that better?"

"Ummm, much," he murmured, capturing her face between his hands and holding her still long enough for his lips to devour hers.

After several minutes of serious "greetings" he bent down and swept her into his arms. Expecting him to carry her to the bedroom for a complete reunion, Jenny was surprised when he headed away from the house, not stopping until they stood next to the new pickup truck. Setting her down inside the back, he climbed in next to her and pulled her onto his lap.

"So how do you like our new truck?"

"*Our?*"

"Yes, I bought it this afternoon. We'll need it for the ranch. I don't want to speak poorly of Bob, but he needs a rest." Garrett ran his hand over the new truck's smooth paint. "I thought we might name it Dave unless you have a better idea."

"No, Dave will be fine. But I think I must have missed something. I just got back from the docks and the man told me you and Pete had sailed this morning."

"He was half right. *Pete* sailed this morning, but I decided to stay behind. It seems that during my stay here, some crazy, beautiful, unpredictable, adorable young woman clipped my wings and I couldn't fly away like I'd planned."

"You're not going to the Caribbean?"

"Not anytime soon. Unless you would like to go there on our honeymoon."

"Honeymoons usually follow weddings," Jenny commented casually.

"And weddings usually follow proposals." Lifting her hand to his lips he said, "Miss Jennifer Grant, also known as the Wild Woman, may I have the honor of having your hand, as well as the rest of your gorgeous body, in holy matrimony? I'm afraid I don't have a rock with me to make into a ring, but maybe tomorrow we could go to Corpus and pick something out."

Jenny looked up at him, wishing she could say yes, but there were still too many questions without answers. "But what will we do when you go to a new job? I can go with you for a short time, but I really couldn't stay away long."

"I didn't think you would ever be able to give this place up, but I decided not to take that personally. I gave it a lot of thought last night and knew it wasn't fair of me to force you into making a choice. And I'm sorry for what I said, because I know how deeply you love this land and your animals. I can only hope you have room in your life for one more."

"But your job . . ."

"I've made a slight career change. Sea-Free offered me the position of facility director and I've taken it. I'll be responsible for coordinating the studies of the fish and animals there, and will oversee all the experimentation, especially with the white whales. The pay is excellent and the work is what I love to do."

She studied his blue eyes intently, searching for any hint of disappointment. "Are you sure? I would never ask you to give up anything you truly love."

He grinned his lopsided, infinitely tender grin she had come to know so well. "I truly love you, my lovely Jenny. And I couldn't be happy if I had to give you up."

"But Pete and the sailboat?"

"Pete bought out my interest in *The Eagle and The Hawk*. I guess he'll have to rename it *The Hawk* because the eagle is ready to nest . . . that is, if I've found my mate. I still haven't heard your answer."

Jenny wrapped her arms around his neck and snuggled closer. "Eagles mate for life, you know."

"I can live with that."

"But you love the sea. Won't you miss the freedom?"

"You and I can buy a small sailboat and we can slip away for a few days whenever we want to."

"And your trip around the world?"

"You can go with me. And when we have little eaglets, they can go, too."

"I think we already have a not so little eaglet. Rusty's going to stay here permanently if we can work out a deal with his stepfather."

"Good. He's a terrific kid and I think the three of us will make a good beginning for our family."

"Well, I've given you every chance to back out," Jenny said. "So it's too late now. Yes, I happily accept your proposal. I would be very proud to become your wife. I'm sorry about your boat and your trip, but I love you very much and the thought that you had left me forever was awful."

"I'll never leave you," he promised, his breath warm against her face as their lips met again in a long, hungry kiss. "Unless you want to initiate this truck, why don't we finish this discussion in the house."

She nodded her consent and let him help her climb back over the side. As they walked toward the house with their arms wrapped around each other, Jenny commented, "You seem pretty sure of yourself. You would have been stuck with a pickup truck if I had said no. So how did you know I was wildly, madly in love with you?"

He squeezed her tighter and admitted, "I didn't. But I took the chance, knowing that you can't turn away a stray. If you hadn't said yes, I would have hung around your back porch, looking pitiful and begging for your attention until you changed your mind."

Tilting her head, she flashed him an adoring smile. "You, my love, will never have to beg."